Dying Innocence

By David Alex Fleming

Copyright © 2011 DAVID ALEX FLEMING

All rights reserved.

ISBN:146098854X
ISBN-13:978-1460988541

In Memoriam, Earl R. Palmer, L.L.B.

1929-1994

"Old Lawyers Never Die,

They Just Loose Their Appeal"

Introduction

The witch trials of the 1600's cost many women their lives. It was believed that these women were possessed by the devil. During their trials, witnesses would testify that they **seen** actions and **heard** sounds consistent with that of a possessed person. They would be sentenced to death and executed before the cheers of the town.

For hundreds of years, eye witness

testimony has been the most reliable form of proof ever offered in a court of law. After all, seeing is believing, or is it?

In the 1940's, Jim Watson, then a graduate student, discovered the existence of DNA and in the 1980's, Watson worked with a group of others to develop a human genetic sequence as it relates to genetic transfer of diseases in hopes that he could eliminate the gene that causes the transfer. Not knowing it at the time, they would later set the stage for use of DNA in criminal cases. The use of DNA as evidence in criminal cases would forever change the way we think of eye witness testimony.

Since the late 80's, early 90's, hundreds of people facing death row after eye witness testimony secured their conviction have been found to be totally innocent and released from incarceration. Before DNA was used however, many had lost their lives having been convicted of a horrific crime they didn't commit.

This is the story of one of those men, welcome to Dying Innocence!

Dying Innocence

DYING INNOCENCE

Chapter 1

"Let's have one more beer before we take off guys," Kevin said as he waived over the

Waitress. "So Dale, what are you going to have?"

"I will have another haps light, Kev," Dale said.

"What about you Steve?"

"Hey, get me a haps light too; I'm going to the restroom, be right back fellas," Steve said as he headed back to the head. The waitress took Kevin's order and went to get it. "I can't believe I got drunk tonight, I have to be at work at six-thirty," Dale said shaking his head.

"Awe, now this won't be the first time," Kevin replied. The men laughed.

The waitress brought them three more mugs of beer and another bowl of peanuts. "That will be six dollars Kevin," she said holding out her hand.

Steve come out of the restroom and walked over to the jukebox to play a song. After he finished with the music, he took a seat back at the table to finish his drink. "On the count of three, one, two, three." Everybody downed their beers and got up to head out. Kevin left the waitress a small tip and got his coat.

"You all ready?" Steve asked as he was putting his coat on.

The three men headed out the door of the Fox Club and started to get in Kevin's new car. "You guys wait, I need to take a leak!" Dale said. He walked back behind the dumpster so nobody would see him. Kevin and Steve got in the car to get it started so they could get some heat on. It was only five degrees above zero. That's normal for January in Clark County, Indiana. Some folks would consider that five degrees to be a warm front compared to the below zero weather they had the last two weeks or so.

" Ahhhhh, SHIT, ahhhhh, ahhhhh," Dale screamed from behind the dumpster.

"Man, what the hell is wrong with him," Kevin asked setting in the driver's seat of the car.

"He must have zipped his shit up!" Steve said. They started laughing. "Here, I will get out and see what's going on!" Steve said opening the door and standing half way out of the car.

Steve looked over to the dumpster but didn't see Dale anywhere. "Dale, where the hell you at man?" Everything was dark and quite. "Come on man, stop playing around, its cold out here dude." Steve got out and shut the door to Kevin's car. Having called out and gotten no response from Dale, He walked back to see what was keeping him. As he went around the dumpster, he could see Dale bent down looking at something. "Hey, what's that Dale?" Dale didn't say anything. Steve began to walk closer. As he walked towards Dale, he could see a pale white leg that appeared to have blood on it. "What the hell is that Dale?" Steve asked in a bit of shock.

"It's a naked girl, she won't answer me," Dale replied.

"O my god, come on Dale, let's get the hell out of here man, that girl is probably dead. They will think we did it dude. Steve reached down and tried to pull Dale up.

"Somebody just left this poor girl out here with no clothes on to die; I'm calling the cops Steve." Dale walked over to a pay phone in the parking lot of the bar and dialed for the operator.

"Yes, we need the Police out here to the Fox Club right away!"

"Please hold on the line while I put you though sir," the operator said to Dale'

Dale waited in the cold while she connected him.

The call came into the Emergency Dispatch Center of the Clark County Sheriff's Department. The date was recorded in the log as January Twenty-fifth at two am.

"Yes, ah, my name is Dale Moss, and I'm not exactly sure, but I believe there's a girl out here at the Fox Club, hurt pretty bad. She's laying out back by the dumpster, Moss said as he looked to the girl from a distance."

"Is she breathing Sir?"

"I don't know, I'm not getting close to her, she is naked and has blood all over her."

"We are sending officers to that location now, we ask that you remain on location until we arrive Mr. Moss," the dispatcher said as she put out the call. "Fire one, we have an emergency at the Fox Club, a person is down near the dumpster, condition unknown. Possible homicide or criminal activity involved. Please await law enforcement before entering scene."

"10-4, this is fire one, response time, ten minutes." The alarms started ringing in the fire station. The big doors opened to the front of the fire house and trucks come out with their emergency lights flashing and sirens blasting. "Medic One, we are in route to the Fox Club."

Clark County Sheriff John Matts was called at home by the dispatcher at around Two Ten am. Sheriff Matts is known around town as an aggressive cop who goes to the edge to get his man. Matts lost a son in nineteen seventy nine to a drunk driver and became a deputy sheriff that year. Many people in Clark County say Matts was a little too aggressive because of an incident that happened at a bar a few years back. Matts had struck a man in the bar who many say was just being drunk and loud rather than resisting. Matts was never charged for any crime or cited for any official misconduct regarding the incident.

Sheriff Matts left his house and got in his patrol car. He heard a Deputy calling for him.

"Sheriff, you there?" Deputy James Morgan called out.

"Yes Jimmy, what have you got out there? Matts replied.

"Well John, I think we're dealing with a fatality here, ah, probably a murder John!"

"You all wait until I get there Jimmy, don't do anything but crowd control, I will call down to dispatch and have Jen call the Coroner!" Sheriff Matts ordered as he turned on his emergency lights and shot out County Road 150 East towards the club.

Matts pulled up to the parking lot of the Fox Club and seen the Coroners van right behind him. All the spotlights from the patrol cars where on pointing at the scene. Sheriff Matts got out of his car; he could see what appeared to be the naked body of a teenaged girl. As Matts walked towards the body, a sick feeling came over him as the face of the young lady became more and more recognizable.

"O my god, that's Abby Star, Judge Star's granddaughter!"

"Looks like she's been raped John," observed Coroner Bob Johnson.

"We better get this one right boys, now you get on the horn to Jen and have her call Judge Star, and, better call and wake up the prosecutor and get him down here too."

"Jimmy, I want to know every person that was in that bar tonight, and I'm going to want to interview the Bartender down at the station house," Matts instructed.

"Ok Sheriff, I'm headed in the bar now." Jimmy replied.

The Coroner loaded the body for transport to the lab as Sheriff Matts bagged undergarments, blood and semen samples, and a hair found under the nail of the victim's right hand.

Matts knew he had a major task ahead of him. He had to get this case solved fast; otherwise, his days as Sheriff could be limited. The publicity this case would bring, being a rape and murder of a Judges Granddaughter in a small town would be substantial and will call for pause, patients, and professionalism, Matts thought as he left for the station.

Sheriff Matts arrived on station to interview the Bartender, and, hopefully to get some preliminary information from the Coroner on the cause of death. As he pulled up, he saw a lot of press. His pulse began to beat faster. He knew it was going to be intense the moment he stepped out of his car.

"Sheriff Matts, if I could get a word with you? "A Reporter from the Daily Record asked.

"I'm sorry, but, I can't answer any questions at this time, I will address the press when I have more Information," Matts replied.

As Matts walked in the door, he notice people everywhere. Matts could not remember a time when the Sheriff's Office was more jam-packed. At the end of the hall, Matts could see Judge Star holding his Daughter.

"John, what can you tell me about this?" Judge Star asked with a look of despair on his face.

"We don't know the answer to that just yet Judge, I will need to review the Coroner's report are waiting for the preliminary medical report from the Coroner," Matts replied.

"What can you tell me about the crime scene John?" Judge Star asked.

"It appears that your Granddaughter was murdered, and, there is some indication of rape, although, we have not confirmed that just yet. I can tell you that there was sexual activity." Matts regretted to say.

"Do you have any suspects yet?" Judge Star asked.

"Not at the present time, you're Honor." Matts replied.

"John, did she suffer, I mean, was she made to suffer long do you know?" Judge Star asked as his Daughter began to lose it.

"I don't know enough to determine those facts." Matts replied.

"You get the bastards who did this John, you hear me, you get em!" the Judge ordered pointing his finger.

"Yes Sir, I will do my best Sir." Matts replied, putting his hand on the Judges shoulder.

Matts was upset as he seen the look of utter despair on the faces of the Judge and his Daughter. He headed downstairs to the restroom to compose himself a bit before anyone noticed he was taking it all personally. The last thing he wanted to do was appear unprofessional with the press standing everywhere just waiting to snap a shot of him for the front page of the newspaper. It's clear that this was Sheriff Matt's first big case and his nerves were working him over a bit. Matts washed his face and went back upstairs to interview the Bartender. Chief Deputy Arlin Hants was standing in the dispatch room waiting on the Sheriff to come back up.

"What the hell are we dealing with here John?" Hants asked

walking up to the Sheriff.

"We found the body of Abby Star outside the Fox Club tonight, and, I'm about to go interview the Bartender. We are going to interview a lot of people and I'm going to need you to conduct some of them Arlin." Matts instructed.

"Ok John, I'm going to set in on this one if you don't mind, let me grab a recording device, be right in." Hants replied.

"Good morning, my name is Sheriff John Matts, and you are?" Matts said as he took a seat across the table.

"Dale Row."

"Do you mind if we record this interview?" Matts requested. Deputy Hants set a recorder on the table and started to turn it on.

"No, not at all."

"Mr. Row, you were the Bartender at the Fox Club tonight, is that correct?"

"Yes Sir, I worked the night shift."

"I'm going to ask you to recall anything unusual that may have happened last night; can you do that for me?"

"Well Sir, it was an ordinary night, nothing really unusual about it."

"Did you notice anyone coming and going for example?"

"Not really, I do remember John Miller coming in last night about Nine-Thirty; he was acting kind of upset about something which is kind of unusual I guess."

"Did he appear to have any blood on him that you could see?"

"Not that I could see, it was pretty busy, I do remember that he had a few beers and left, he didn't say anything to anyone."

"Ok Dale, that's all I have for now, give us a call if you remember anything else after you have had time to rest." Matts instructed.

"Sheriff, you have a call on line five, it's the Medical Examiner," the dispatcher informed. Matts headed over to a phone.

"Lay it on me Coroner, what are we dealing with?" Matts said as he pulled out his pen and paper.

" Well John, the girl smells of beer, but I couldn't find any in her system, she was raped for sure, we found sexual fluids, believed to be from a man, in three locations of the body, and, we found a black hair that does not belong to her stuck in her hair. It appears from our initial review of the body that the cause of death is strangulation given the blue cast to the lips and nails, however that is only a preliminary finding"

"Do you think it was more than one person Coroner?" Matts asked, writing as fast as he could.

"Don't know just yet John, I will have to get back to you on that."

Sheriff Matts headed out to his patrol car to go home. It had been a very long and emotional night. Matts was tired and needed to get some rest. As he pulled up to his driveway, he noticed his wife Sara waiting on the porch for him. Matts knew she would be. She had always been supportive like that.

"You ok babe?" Sara asked as she put her hand to the side of his face.

"I'm not sure, I mean, my god Sara, what a night."

"I made you some meatloaf and mashed potatoes. There in the oven keeping warm." Sara walked out to the kitchen to open the oven.

"Great, I'm going to eat and get some sleep." Matts walked out to the kitchen and had a seat at the table. He was hungry, but, just couldn't eat. He took off towards the bedroom." Let me know if anyone calls, ok babe?" Matts said as he got in bed.

"Ok, I just made the bed so; it should be cool, just like you like it." Sara covered him up and shut the light out.

It was about nine-thirty at night and John could hear the phone ringing. He heard Sara run to the phone so it didn't wake him up.

"Babe, it's Arlin on the phone." Sara said with the door creped open.

John got out of bed and answered the phone next to the bed. "Yes Arlin, what's up?"

"We got a witness down here, said she seen John Miller standing around the dumpster in back of the Fox Club acting really strange." Matts grabbed a pen and wrote down the name, John Miller.

"Pull his record and see if we have a current address on him."

"Already did, he don't have a record but I got his address from driving records. He lives on Maryville Road, just a half mile from the bar."

"I will meet you at the station; give me a few minutes Arlin." Matts said as he was pulling his pants up to his waist.

Matts went to meet Hants and they went out to the Millers property. As they pulled into the driveway, they could hear music coming from the house. There were no lights on with the exception of a room to the back of the house. They got out and approached the rear window to the old country house. As they got closer, they heard the sounds of someone having sex, em, o my, mm. They looked in the window and saw a naked blonde headed girl bouncing up and down. She had to be pretty young given her small frame. They could see a man lying on his back and other women covering his face with her body. The small breasted blonde girl bent down and kissed the large breasted girl as they both continued to ride the male. "Well, what do you know, he is in to young girls Sheriff," Hants said looking in the window.

"Yes he is Arlin; do you know either of the girls in there?

"The black haired girl looks like Kim, ah, shit; I can't remember the last name. Matts moved over to get a better look at the room around them.

"He has black hair Sheriff," noticed Hants.

"Let's go back to the car Arlin; I don't want them to notice us out here. Get the plate numbers to that car setting in the driveway; I want to know who that young girl is." Matts and Hants slowly walked back to the patrol car. Hants wrote the plate number down and they pulled out without any lights on.

Chapter 2

Jonny Miller was a laid back, quite person. He never caused any problems as a kid or as an adult. The town generally thought good of John, and, that's saying something. There's not a of people in Clark County who could be described that way, at least as it relates to their childhood.   Growing up in Clark County Indiana was great, but, like most small towns, there was not much for kids to do, leaving open the opportunity to get in some trouble. John did have another side that went unrecognized by the general public. He went to college to get an education, and, returned as an expert of the great party. Like most people his age, he had a thing for women and booze. He obtained his degree from Arlington University in nineteen eighty. He received a B.S. in Liberal Arts Education with Honors. His G.P.A. was nearly perfect at 3.9 out of 4.0. He was born and raised in Clark County. His parents, Drs. Mark and Kateland Miller, both had a medical practice in town for over twenty years. John had a sister named Amy. She was well known by a lot of people in the small city. Amy didn't get that great education like the rest of the family; she dropped out of college after her first year. She has been in and out of jail and is known generally as a drunk. Amy's criminal history really amounts to problems with drugs.

The last time Amy spent time in jail, she met a girl by the name of Kim Lang. Amy brought Kim over to Johns house for a party about two years ago, and, John and Kim hit it off from day one. They got married in June of nineteen eighty two after only Six months of courtship. Kim was very pretty with long dark hair and a small frame. She had unusually large breast for her size. There were some in the Miller family that didn't share John's excitement about the union. Johns Mother Kateland had been critical of Kim from the day they met. Kim had a wild side to her that was obvious from the first time she opened her mouth. She was foul mouthed and sexually expressive. She didn't care much who didn't like it; it was just the way she was.

The first year John met Kim, he brought her to the Miller family reunion. It was the first time anybody in the family had met her. She had on a half shirt with no brawl, clearly exposing the bottom of her breasts and a pair of cut off shorts that didn't leave much to the imagination. Talk about a shocker, the men at the reunion were pre-occupied with her most of the day. The women were pre-occupied watching the men watch her. Every time she bent down to grab something, or, jumped in the air to catch that soccer ball, the men's heads all moved to the beat. As you might imagine, it caused a bit of problem for the women at the reunion, For the Miller family, it was all a bit embarrassing, never the less, it was a problem that the men would look forward to each year thereafter, as sad as that may sound.

John came back to Clark County after college and landed a job with the Clark County School Corp. as a Substitute Teacher. He had plans on going to Graduate School and getting a Doctor of Pharmacy degree once he got a few years of work in. Until then, John took a second job at Lilly's Drug Store as a Pharmacy Tech.

"Come on John, its Six Thirty," Kim said as John began moving around in bed.

"Did you make coffee yet?"

"Yes, there's some making now."

" Come over her sexy girl," John said as he pulled at her panties." Let me have that hot little body this morning!"

"No tiger, you are almost late for class, did you forget that you had to teach today?"

"Well, sometimes it's hard to keep up with what I'm doing from one day to the next." John lay back and covered his head with a pillow. "I could call in sick?" he said as he watched her bounce around with nothing but panties on. She gave him the, I'm not even in the mood look. "Ok, I'm getting up sweetie." John said reluctantly.

John got out of bed and headed to the shower. Kim went into the kitchen and made a quick breakfast. It was going to be a crazy day for John; he had to teach until three, then, go to the Dentist for a cleaning, and then help his best friend move. It was also test day at school. It was always crazy on test day. Students were always shitty.

John left the house for work around Seven Thirty and decided to stop by the Coffee Connection for a cup of joe. He entered the coffee shop and saw an old Friend standing in line waiting to be served.

"Hey John, got class today, I assume."

"Well, it is damn test day, what's you up to, headed to work?"

"Well, needed some coffee, woke up a little late today."

"You woke up a little late, or, you're late because you were getting a little?"

"Well, seems like you know me a little too good Jonny."

"Must be nice Rex."

"Hey John, what was that Sheriff car doing at your house the other night?"

"That Sheriff, what Sheriff? there was no Sheriff at my house that I know of!"

"The hell you say, I know that cop car anywhere, I work on it down at the shop all the time. It belongs to the Sheriff himself."

"That's all news to me Rex, but, I will look into it."

John could not figure out why the Sheriff would be at his house. After a moment, he remembered that that's the night Kim talked him into a threesome. The music was really blasting and they all were in the bedroom doing the deed. I bet they were there for the loud music, John thought to himself.

As John arrived for class, he noticed a big poster of Abby Star in the front yard of the School. On it, it said, WE WILL MISS YOU VERY MUCH. When he got to the office, he noticed that a meeting was going on that he didn't know about over in the teachers' lounge. John snuck in around the back in case he missed the memo on the meeting.

"As you all know, Abby Star was killed a few days ago; they found her down by the Fox Club. They believe she had been raped but we don't know that for sure. Now, there are a lot of students who knew Abby and they are going to be upset. Many of them will have questions and we need to make sure that they get to their counselors office if they do. So if any students seem to be displaying stress over the incident, send them to counseling today, we also have decided to move up test day until later in the week so this incident don't get in the way of their scores. If nobody has anything else...., ok, that's all then, thank you." Dean Richmond said.

Nine Thirty in the morning, Clark County Sheriff's Office. Sheriff Matts was on the phone with Henry Leeman, County D.A.

"Mr. Leeman, we are still investigating as you know, but, we are closing in on some really good leads."

"Tell me what you got so far John?"

"Well Sir, we have information that a local fella, John Miller, was seen around the dumpster at the Fox Club the night of the murder.

We also have found out through our investigation that Miller lives only a half mile from where the body was found. Also, we found a black hair on the victim's body that matches Millers. My chief Deputy and I went to the Millers to question him about the incident and noticed a loud party going on as we pulled up. We snuck up to a bedroom window and noticed Mr. Miller having sex with a young girl and his wife at the same time. We are running the girls tag now to find out who she is."

"Well hell John, that a whole lot more than I thought you would have, now, have you questioned Miller, what does he say about it all?"

"We have not interviewed the Millers just yet; I thought it would be a good idea to get some evidence on him with these young girls, possibly a sting operation or something."

"Well, that's a good idea, not the sting, but, getting the sex habits on tape. That will go a long way with a jury. What about the victim, was she drinking in the bar that night?"

"No, the toxicology report indicated no booze, but the Coroner could smell it on her body. It did say that she had drugs in her system. The night that we were at John Millers house, there was beer cans everywhere."

"Where does Miller meet these girls?" "Wait a minute, isn't he a teacher at the high school?"

"Yes, and, he also works down at the drug store."

"So Miller meets these girls in class, brings them home for sex with his wife, and drugs them up from the drugs he takes at the drug store, rapes the girls, and in this case, murdered the girl to keep her quite. John, I think you got this case figured out. I think I can establish probable cause for a search warrant on the Millers home. Don't worry about getting the sex habits on tape, your testimony really should be enough. I want you to get the witness in there who saw Miller by the dumpster that night, and, get her to elaborate on what it was she saw. I think you have enough to charge him John, go ahead and pick him up on a preliminary charge of murder."

"Yes Sir, I will have him picked up within the hour."

"I want him incarcerated now because he has access to other girls. No matter if he talks or not, arrests him."

"As you wish Sir, we are headed to get him now."

Chapter 3

One Thirty in the afternoon, Clark Superior Court.

" Court comes to order, show the State present by the Chief Deputy Prosecutor, Tom Kirkson, show also the States Witnesses, Deputy Arlin Hants of the Clark County Sheriff's Department, the Coroner Robert Johnson of the Clark County Medical Examiner's Office, and...Who else you got down there Tom?" Judge Thomas asked.

"That it Judge," Kirkson replied.

"Very well, comes now the State of Indiana and moves the court to consider determination of probable cause for a search warrant and.......is there a request for an arrest warrant at this time Mr. Kirkson?"

" It pleas the court, ah, your Honor, should the court find probable cause for an arrest at this time based on the evidence provided, then yes Judge."

"Mr. Kirkson, either the State request an arrest warrant or they don't,"

"Yes, we do your Honor."

"Very well, you may call your first witness, Mr. Kirkson."

"State calls Deputy Arlin Hants to the stand."

"Please tell the court your name and rank please."

"My name is Chief Deputy Arlin Hants. I am with the Clark County Sheriff's Office."

"Would you tell the court your findings in this matter?"

"As part of our investigation of the death of Nineteen year old Abby Star, we obtained a statement from Fran Keller, who told us that she observed John Miller next to a dumpster at the Fox Club, just a few feet from the body. She observed his behavior as strange. Thereafter, we matched a hair found on the body of the victim to that of John Miller. We then obtained a statement from the Bartender of the Fox Club who saw John Miller at the Club that night, again, acting strange. Our investigation turned up evidence that Miller lives only a half mile away from where the body was found and that Mr. Miller enjoys having sex with young girls from the school he teaches at. Millers wife also joins in on the sex sessions."

"Now, that last part, how do you know about the sex parties, and, was there beer at these parties?"

"The Sheriff and I went to the Millers property and looked in a rear window where we noticed John Miller laying on his back, a young girl having sexual intercourse with him, and, also, Mr. Miller's wife was getting oral sex by Mr. Miller all at the same time. There were beer cans everywhere."

"Now, did you notice any smell on the victim?"

"Yes, she smelled like beer."

"Ok, is there anything else?"

"Yes, we discovered that John Miller has a second job at Lilly's Drug Store where we believe he got the drugs found in the victims system."

The Court, "That's enough Tom; I don't need any more evidence. Court hears the evidence and finds probable cause for the search of the Miller property as well as the arrest of John Miller. Let the record reflect, State of Indiana vs. John Miller, cause number............49D01-8301-CF-442. Court orders the defendant arrested and brought before this court and to answer to a preliminary charge of murder. Court sets bond at.........well; this is a murder trial, court orders NO BOND.

Is there anything further Mr. Kirkson?"

"That's all I have Judge, thank you."

John Miller was on his way to lunch when he heard his name come across the intercom. He headed down to the office and could see cops everywhere.

"You John Miller?" asked a Deputy.

"I am."

" You are under an arrest for the murder of Abby Star, please place your hands behind your back, you have the right to remain silent, anything you say can and will be held against you in a court of law, you have the right to an attorney, if you cannot afford one, one will be provided for you.

"What the hell are you talking about, have you lost your mind, what's this about?"

"We will explain everything to you when we get to the station John."

"Is this some kind of joke," Miller said as his heart began to beat fast.

The staff at the school gave John a look he would never forget. It was at that time that he finally realized, this was no joke, he was being arrested for murder. As he left, the teaching staff all come walking down the halls looking at John in shock and dismay. Once they got to the station, John was put in a room with a table and three chairs. Now, John's heart was racing out of his chest. Sheriff Matts walked in along with Chief Deputy Arlin Hants.

"Are you going to talk or not Miller?"

"Talk about what, I didn't do anything."

"It would be wise for you to come clean and tell us about the girl, look, was it a sexual thing that had gone bad, or what?"

"I don't know what you are talking about, but I want to call my Lawyer."

"Fine, lock him up Arlin; we have already secured a warrant for his arrest," ordered the Sheriff.

John Miller was taken to the jail and booked in for murder. They made him take all his clothes off and sprayed his hair and body with bug spray that burned like hell. He was told to take a shower and return to a bench outside the shower. He got out and waited for some clothes to put on. A female Corrections Officer unlocked the door and asked him to stand up. She asked him to turn his naked body around and watched as he did. It was the most horrible thing John ever had to do.

"He's a medium Kelly," she stated on the intercom.

"10-4," replied the guard.

"You can just have a seat right they on that bench." she ordered.

A few minutes later, another female Guard entered the room and told him to stand up, she handed him a set of jail clothes and watched him get dressed.

"Do female guards always watch male inmates take showers in here?"

"Get used to it sweetie, welcome to jail!"

John was taken to a small holding cell where he would set for Three days. Finally, a guard came to the little five inch by five inch window and told John that they were going to get him out for a shower and phone call. The loud metal door opened.

" Step out and walk to the shower room," the female guard said." John walked over to the shower room and waited on instructions to go ahead and get in the shower.

"Ok inmate, remove your clothing and through them in the blue basket and get your shower, you have Eight minutes."

John was having a hard time with this whole jail thing. The food was really bad, female guards watched you take showers, even when you go to the bathroom. You set in a blank green cell with nothing to do but think about what is happening to you, and, just when you want to lay down and go to sleep to escape the madness, the other inmates are slamming shit up against the walls and making all kinds of noise like animals. It was all enough to make you break down and loose it. Anybody who would commit a crime, knowing they were coming in here for it, had to be a real dummy. The only thing that kept some sanity in Johns mind is the fact that he knows he is innocent, and, it will all be over soon.

"Your Eight minutes are up, step out here now please. Here are your clean clothes, get dressed and let's hurry it up if you want to make a phone call."

John put the clothes on and waited on the guard to take him to the phone for his call. A guard called for him to step out.

"You have five minutes to make a phone call."

John picked up the phone and called his father. "Dad, you're not going to believe this, I'm in jail for murder."

"Well, I heard that you were arrested, there was a big story in the newspaper, I'm waiting on Gavin Palmer to get back from his vacation today so I can get him on your case, how are you holding up in there?"

"I will be ok, I guess they think I raped and killed Abby Star, I don't really know."

"It will be alright John, you didn't do it, and so, just hang tight, and I'm calling Palmer after lunch."

"Ok Dad, I'm sorry I had to call you in the office, but, I have to make a call when they tell me to."

"Gavin will be in there to see you and we will visit on visiting day, do you need some money put on your books?"

"I don't know what I would do with money in here, but, if I need any, I will lets you know at visiting, well, my Five minutes is up, got to go, love you Dad."

"Love you to John, you just hang on, were going to get you out of there."

The guard escorted John back to the little green cell and shut the big metal door.

Chapter 4

People in the courts and especially those in the Clark County Prosecutors Office hated hearing the name Gavin Palmer Esq. Gavin Palmer had been a defense lawyer in Clark County for years. He was known as the best of the best. He was a big, loud, guy that didn't take any shit from anyone, not even the judges that have come and went. Palmer shocked many people with his assertive stare and his direct personality. You could say he had a serious attitude problem, but, he got the job done never the less. He reminded you of the old Perry Mason type of lawyer. There were not too many lawyers around these days like that. He was exact on facts and procedures. Nothing got by him at all. When you have a case and the lawyer on the other side is Gavin Palmer, you had better do your homework and even add to your staff because to do any less would cost you the case. In fact, out of all the years Palmer has been in practice, he has lost three cases. The great thing about Gavin Palmer was that he didn't buddy-up with the other lawyers and judges. Palmer always said that to do so would be a great disservice to your client.

"Palmer Law Office, may I help you?" the secretary answered.

"Yes, this is Dr. Mark Miller, and, I was calling back to speak to Gavin Palmer."

"Let me see if I can get him on the phone for you."

"Gavin Palmer here, what can I do for you Dr. Miller?"

"I wanted to retain your services for my son, John Miller."

"What's the charge Doc?"

"Well, he's being charged with rape and ah, murder."

"Seriously, where's he at now?"

"He's in jail."

"You got to be kidding me, what's it about? I'm sorry but, I've been on vacation and I'm not up to speed on current events."

"He's being charged for the rape and murder of Abby Star. He's being held without bail."

"Abby Star! any relation to the judge?"

"Yes, I think so, a granddaughter."

"Does your son have a criminal record of any kind Dr. Miller?"

"No, he's never been in trouble in his life. He teaches at the high school."

"Has he been to court yet?"

"Not unless they took him up there this afternoon."

"What is the evidence against him, do they even have any at all?"

"Well, he didn't do it so, whatever they do have is false, if they have anything at all."

"Dr. Miller, I will need a pretty large retainer on this type of a case."

"I will have whatever you need sent over to your office."

"Ok, I will go see John at the jail, and then I will come by tonight, are you and Kateland going to be home tonight?"

"We will make it a point to be!"

"Fine, I will see you then," Palmer said as he hung up the phone.

Palmer gathered his briefcase and headed for the door. "Darla, I'm on my way to the jail, see you in the morning," Palmer said to his secretary.

Clark County Sheriff's Office, Palmer rushed through the door like a pro-bowl linebacker in the NFL.

"Where's that damn Sheriff at?" Palmer demanded of the dispatcher.

"I will call him for you Sir," explained the dispatcher.

"Hey, that's a good idea, you do that, and you tell him that Gavin Pal......."

"I know who you are Sir, I'm calling him now, you can have a seat if you would like, and he's not on station."

Palmer remained standing there starring at her like he was about to bum rush the office. The Dispatcher called the Sheriff;

"Sheriff Matts, you are wanted on-station."

"What's up? I'm in a meeting right now."

"Gavin Palmer is here to see you about John Miller."

"Shit, you got to be kidding me, Palmer huh!"

"Do you want me to tell him to wait, or, should I try to set an appointment with him?"

"No, I'm in route now."

"He seems to be upset, Sheriff."

"No, that's just Gavin Palmer; I will see you in a few."

Sheriff Matts rubbed his head as he thought to himself, out of all the damn lawyers, he had to get Palmer. Matts headed over to the station. He knew he was about to jump into the pit. Matts had already dealt with Palmer on a few matters in the past, it was pretty damn ugly. After that, Matts made it a policy to avoid that crazy son of a bitch at any costs. The problem here is that he was representing a murder suspect. He had to answer his questions by law. As Matts pulled into the Sheriff's Office, he could see Palmer standing at the big glass door starring out at him. Matts got goose bumps just seeing his fat face.

"What's the deal here Matts?"

"Well, Mr. Palmer, we did arrest John Miller, and, I want you to know that we have only carried out the orders of the Prosecutors Office and the Clark Superior Court."

"Of course you are, going to put it all on someone else huh?, your telling me you didn't have anything to do with it, just following orders like a good little trooper huh?, you didn't investigate this bullshit?"

"Well we....."

"Did you arrest my client on a warrant?"

"Yes, out of Superior Court!"

"John Miller is not to be questioned without my being present, and even then, we will answer no questions!"

"Yes Sir, we have not asked him any questions yet?"

"Yet, you aren't going to ask him nothing Matts, you got me? nothing."

Palmer turned around and walked out. Matts wiped the sweat off his forehead and went to his office. He called the Prosecutors Office to let them know that Gavin the madman Palmer has taken the case.

Palmer went over to the jail to see John Miller, the Sheriff said they arrested Miller on a warrant for murder which means they have had a probable cause hearing, and, Judge Thomas found that there was probable cause. This indicated to Palmer that they had to have some evidence against him. Judge Thomas was a States Judge, that is, he's usually for the State in most cases, but, when it came to cases like this, he would have made damn sure the State had some evidence to support the warrant. Not so much because he worries about innocent people getting convicted, but rather, because cases like this tend to generate a lot of publicity and he's about as political as they get. Judge Thomas could be seen from time to time talking crazy to Defense Attorney's in court. He was a Prosecutor before running for Judge and it never really changed the way he thinks. The law is about role playing to a great extent. A Prosecutor thinks like a Prosecutor, and a Defense Lawyer thinks like a Defense Lawyer, and the Judge, is to be the balance of the two. It does not always work out that way; in fact, it never really works that way in the modern age of the practice of the law. Palmer walked into the jail and showed the Jailer his bar card and asked to see John Miller. He walked over to counsel room, a room for lawyers to see their clients, and waited for Miller.

"Have a seat there John, my name is Gavin Palmer and I will be representing you in this case. I was hired by your father."

"Thank you for taking the case, I'm so glad to have someone on my side for a change."

"Are you doing ok in here, are these assholes giving you any problems?"

"No, I'm not worried about them; I just want to get out of here."

"Well, that tells me you are innocent."

"What does?"

"You telling me you just want to get out of here, you see John, when someone is guilty of the crime they are being charged with and incarcerated on, the last thing they are thinking about is getting out, they are thinking about how fast they can get a deal, so that, eventually, they can get out. When you were doing this as long as I have, you pick up on these things. Now, tell me what you know about this whole thing?"

"I don't know anything, they came to the school and arrested me for the murder of some girl, put me in a little cell, and I've been setting there ever since."

"You don't know the girl at all?"

"Not that I remember, unless I teaches a class she was in?"

"Well, I will find out what it's all about John, you just try to get by in this rat trap."

"I'm trying."

"You say you have been in a little holding cell the whole time you have been in here?"

"Yes, it's about to drive me nuts."

"I will take care of that, I'm going to go, but I will see you in court."

"When will I go to court?"

"I'm not sure; I have to check with the clerk in the morning."

"See you then, and, thank you Mr. Palmer."

Palmer called over to Dr. Miller's house to let them know he would not be coming over due to the late hour. He got some dinner, turned the TV on, and went through the newspapers to find the story on Abby Star. Having just got back from vacation, the papers were stacked at the front door. He looked for the evening paper on

January Twenty-Six. There was a small story about the crime, but, nothing much more. That could only be expected, the investigation had just begun. He went to the paper issued on February First.

"An Arrest was made late yesterday in the murder of Nineteen year old Abby Star, the granddaughter of local Judge Alvin Star. Prosecutors contend that John Miller, a Teacher at Clark High School had met the victim in a social studies class he taught. Prosecutors believe that Miller gave the victim drugs, raped, and then murdered the young girl on January Twenty-Fifth of this year. Police say an unidentified witness seen Miller near where the body was found in the back of the Fox Club. Miller's wife is also considered a suspect, but, police refused to comment any further. The Prosecutor's Office said that Miller will be in court very soon for an initial hearing on a preliminary charge of murder. They also indicated that they would seek the death penalty in the case if found guilty. The Clark County Sheriff's Office investigated the case." `The Daily Record.`

Palmer put the paper down and finished eating his meal.

Chapter 5

It was Five am. Palmers alarm went off. He got out of bed and headed to the kitchen to get the morning coffee started. His day always started out the same. He would have coffee, turn the morning national news on, and work on the day's cases that he would have in court that day. There was something about the morning that brought peace of mind. It allowed him to work with clear thought, having gotten a good night's sleep. He got his coffee and headed to the living room to turn the TV on. He pulled out the file on John Miller and opened it up. For the first time in as long as he could remember, he was doing the file work on a file that was nearly blank. It was as if the case had not started yet... He stated thinking, no wonder, it's a brand new case, normally, he would be hired much later in the case, but, it being a murder charge that could result in a death sentence if convicted, it's better to get a head start. He had not even filed his appearance in the case yet. An appearance is a form that Lawyers file to inform the court and all parties involved that he was representing the defendant. He began to work on his appearance; he would probably have an initial hearing in court with John Miller today and figured he had a procedural obligation let everyone know that he was representing John. The National News started and it was always, "The *Morning Show with Tom Price and Anna Reshod brings you the nation's news first.*" It was the same news cast introduction he had heard every morning for at least Five years in a row. This morning's news cast would be different." *Today, we will bring you the story of a young girl from the small town of Clark County Indiana who was raped and killed and left next to a dumpster. A local Teacher has been arrested in the case. We will hear from the Sheriff who investigated that incident.*" Palmer slowly set the paperwork down and tuned in to the TV. He was not a fan of the media when it came to reporting on criminal cases that have not yet been to trial. Besides the arrest itself, it was a substantial step in the direction of establishing guilt before the case had even made it to court. These stories were always one sided, with an interview from Law Enforcement or a Prosecutor, and they never reported the position of the defense. The stories went a long way in grand standing the incident and also created a path for the viewers, who could be potential jurors, to consider the guilt of the accused before the presentation of evidence in court. If nothing else, it would serve to destroy a person's reputation beyond repair. Palmer rushed to find a blank VCR tape so he could record the story. He put the tape in and waited for the segment.

"We now turn our attention to the young girl in Clark County Indiana who was raped and killed. We have Sheriff John Matts in the studio this morning to talk about the incident. Now Sheriff, It's my understanding that this young girl was raped and killed and it is alleged to have been a Teacher from her High School, is that your take on it?"

"That's true, we have a local Teacher in custody at this time, and His name is John Miller."

"Sheriff, we understand that you are still investigating this incident, what can you tell us so far?"

"Well, we received the call in the early morning hours of January Twenty-Fifth, and upon arrival, we found the lifeless body of Nineteen year old Abby Star in the back of a local bar. We interviewed many people that night and one of those witnesses identified John Miller as having been seen near the body. We then found through toxicology reports that the young lady had drugs in her system and discovered that John Miller worked a second Job where he had access to these drugs. Our investigation revealed that Miller had met the victim from a class he taught at the local high school. We discovered that he lived less *than a mile from where the body was found."*

"Do you believe that Miller has done this sort of thing before, are your investigations focused on that at all?"

"Well, we are looking into that; however, our focus at this time is on the case at hand."

"Well Sheriff, our hopes and prayers go out to the family and we wish you the best in your efforts."

"Thank you."

Palmer stopped the tape and got his briefcase. Palmer knew that the story had come alive. He knew it would be like a bomb had gone off through Clark County. People would be talking about the incident now everywhere. Reporters would be coming from everywhere to follow up. Palmer headed over to the courthouse to file his appearance and to get a time for the initial hearing.

"Do you know when an initial will be held on John Miller, Kathy?" Palmer asked the clerk.

"Here in a few minutes, he's being brought over from the jail. Are you representing the case Gavin?"

"Yes, here's my appearance for the case."

"Great, let me take it to the Judge so he knows your appearing for Mr. Miller."

Palmer walked in the courtroom and took a seat at the defense table. Henry Leeman walked in with a whole arm full of cases and slid them down on the plaintiffs table. Leeman looked over and seen Palmer setting at the defense table looking at a file.

"You are representing Mr. Miller Gavin?"

"Yes, that is correct."

"Here is the charging indictment and the probable cause affidavit."

"Very well, thank you."

Palmer looked over the paperwork the prosecutor handed him. The Judge came in the room and took a set at the bench. The court reporter followed and took a seat at her desk.

Court comes to order, 49D01-8301-CF-442, State of Indiana vs. John Miller. Show the defendant present in person and in the custody of the Clark County Sheriff, show the State present by Henry

Leeman, and.......Mr. Palmer, do you have some interest in this case?"

"Yes Judge, I am representing John Miller, my appearance was filed this morning."

"Oh, I see it here Mr. Palmer, sorry about that."

"Not a problem Judge."

"Let the record reflect that the defendant appears with counsel, Gavin Palmer ...now, this matter is set for an initial hearing on a preliminary charge of Felony Murder, and the indictment reads as follows;

That on or about January Twenty Fifth, Nineteen Eighty Three, John Miller did knowing and intentionally kill another human being, to wit; Abby Star, in violation of Indiana Code 35-4-3-2, and done so while committing a felony, to wit; rape, in violation of Indiana Code 35-8-3-1, all of which is against the peace and dignity of the State of Indiana. Court has heard and found probable cause after an evidentiary hearing, and issued a warrant thereafter. Now, Mr. Palmer, does your client wish to enter a plea?"

"Mr. Miller is not guilty your Honor!"

"Very well, court enters a plea of not guilty for the defendant and set this matter for a pretrial hearing on......March Tenth at Two pm, is that going to be acceptable for you both counselors?"

"Works for me Judge!" Palmer said.

"Ok, and Mr. Leeman?"

"That's fine Judge."

"Are there any other matters, Mr. Palmer, Mr. Leeman?"

"I will be filing a motion seeking to establish a bond in this matter, my client has no criminal record and the merits of the State's case are in the least, questionable."

"Let me save you some time, defense orally moves this court to consider bond, defendants motion is DENIED!"

"Well, I would at least like to present argument," Palmer reasoned.

"This is a murder case Mr. Palmer, I am not required to set a bond in matters of murder or treason, and I'm not going to, your motion is denied. Now is there anything else?"

Henry Leeman looked over at Palmer and noticed Palmer pointing his big fat finger at him. Palmer walked over and bent down to Leemans ear, " I don't know how you pulled this shit off Henry, but, you keep this in mind, as soon as I whip your ass in this case, like I do in every case, I'm coming back and filing a malicious prosecution action against you in the state bar."

Palmer turned and walked out the door. He walked across the street to his old Nineteen Sixty Seven Chrysler and headed for the Fox Club. He wanted to get a look at the crime scene. He pulled up and got out. He walked to the dumpster and noticed a few feet away a leaf with what appeared to be blood on it. He put the leaf in a plastic bag and continued looking around. As he turned to walk back to his car, he noticed through a little wooded area the appearance of tire tracks. It was clear upon inspection that these were not only tire tracks, but, tracks from a car that had been stuck in the mud. It was dark when the Sheriff's department investigated the body so they would not have seen the tracks through the woods. Palmer walked back to his car and got his camera and snapped several shots of the area. He could clearly tell that the tire marks were made from a car. He got in his car and drove down to the Millers property, as he pulled up, he seen Kim Miller putting the dog out back on the chain.

"Hi, my name is Gavin Palmer, and I was wondering if you might tell me what your husband was driving the night he went to the bar?"

"Oh, hi Mr. Palmer, it's good to meet you, huh, he was driving his truck, that's all he ever drives. Why do you ask?"

"Just wondering, huh, do you think you can come in to my office in the morning so that we can go over a few things."

"Sure, I can be there, what time did you have in mind?"

"About ten would be great!"

"I will be there, thank you for helping Jonny Mr. Palmer."

Palmer went to his office and called Greg Jordan. Greg was an expert in automotive theory. He asked Greg to go to the Fox Club and take a look at the tire marks. He asked Greg to see if he could identify the marks and send him a report.

Chapter 6

Clark County Sheriff's Office, the next day.

"Sheriff Matts, you have a call on line Three," the dispatcher instructed.

"Sheriff Matts, how may I help you?"

"Sheriff, this is Detective Martin Taylor of the Bulisha Police Department in Bulisha County Kentucky. I wanted to talk to you about an incident we are currently investigating. You see, we are investigating a rape and murder that have apparent similarities to the Abby Star case that you are investigating."

"You don't say?"

"Yes, it seems as though the young girl in our case was gang raped and the physical evidence matches that of your case. A description of the car that the victim was seen in just prior to her death was a car from Albany Indiana, just about ten miles from Clark County."

"Have you established a time of death for your victim Detective?"

"Yes, we believe that to be February First."

"Well, we have had a person in custody charged with that crime, and, the evidence is pretty strong. He would have been incarcerated at the time of your incident. So as you can see, the cases could not be related Detective. If you wish, you can fax me a copy of the file, and, I would be more than happy to take a look at it for you."

"I will do that Sheriff, if you would, give me a call when you have had a chance to review the file."

"Great, thank you Detective."

Matts no longer hung up the phone and the fax machine started shooting out papers. He went over to pick up what seemed like a book. The top page was a black and white photograph of a naked teenaged girl with lots of blood on her. Matts started to look through the paperwork and ran across the preliminary medical report. The initial report indicated that the killer or killers left sexual fluids in and around many areas of the body. It also indicated that there appeared to be marks around the risks and the neck. Matts put the file in a folder and set it on his desk. He then went out and got in his car, and, headed over to the County Medical Examiner's Office. The Medical Examiner had just completed his findings.

"Coroner, what can you tells me now that you have had a chance to complete your examination?"

"Well John, you are not going to want to hear this, but, you know, it seems to me, that we are dealing with a gang rape here."

"What, why do you say that?"

"Well, she had been violated in every area of the body. She had marks on her wrists from being tied up, she had bite marks on her back that did not match the bite marks on her thigh, and, it appears that the person who violated her in one area was extremely large in size, creating large tares, whereas, the person who violated her elsewhere was not so large and thus, did not create as much damage."

"What the hell," Matts said as thought about the Kentucky case to himself.

"I can tell you this John; whoever did this had some real issues."

"So, your examination establishes strangulation as the cause of death?"

"No John, there were marks of strangulation, but it was not the cause of death. The cause of death was due to a lack of blood. It was because of the violent sex. The loss of blood due to the repeated acts of sex is what took her life."

"What are you saying? she was screwed to death?"

"That's my findings, yes."

"Let me get a copy of the report, I need to go see Henry Leeman."

Matts got the report and headed over to the Prosecutors Office. Henry Leemans secretary told Sheriff Matts that Leeman was in court, that, if he wanted, he could wait. Matts took a seat in the waiting room. He started thinking about the similarities between the two cases. What was Gavin Palmer going to do when he found out that they made a mistake? For the first time in the case, Matts came to the realization that they could have the wrong man in jail for murder.

The prosecutor walked in.

"Hey John, what's up?"

"We need to talk!"

Matts and Leeman walked back to his office. Matts explained everything he had learned about the Kentucky case as well as what the Medical Examiner told him. Matts expressed his concern to Leeman that he thinks they could have the wrong man. Leeman acted as if the information didn't change anything.

"Well John, the excessive for that caused the blood loss was probably the result of some instrument used. The bite marks are different because Millers wife was involved and has a different size mouth. It's all part of their freak show life style John, who's to say that a man can't get off many of times?"

"Well, you have to take this case to trial, but it's my reputa......."

"Look John, we have got the right man, what we need is the instrument they used on the Star girl. You need to conduct a search of the Millers property to see if you can locate that evidence. Now that we have bite marks in evidence, we need to bring Kim Miller in and question her. Also, we need to locate and question the girl you seen having sex with the Millers, let's see what she has to say about it."

"Ok, we will serve that search warrant on the Miller property."

"What about the Kentucky case?"

" Get rid of that file, we have our man, that file will only cause trouble, if Palmer gets ahold of it, he will try to use it to establish reasonable doubt."

"Ok, your right, that's what I will do."

"John, I will just go with you on the search."

Sheriff Matts and Henry Leeman left to go search the Millers.

Kim Miller was setting on her porch. All of a sudden, cops came from everywhere. Matts and Leeman got out and walked up to Kim Miller.

"We are here to search this property pursuant to a search warrant," Matts said.

They started searching the house and as they entered the bedroom, Leeman noticed what appeared to be a small suitcase in the closet. He opened it and found a sex kit that contained a large fake penis as well as some vibrators and crèmes used for sexual activity. A look to the back trash can revealed a belt torn in two parts. They seized the items and took Kim Miller in for questioning.

"Mrs. Miller, we have a few questions for you," Matts said.

"I'm not going to answer any of you damn questions without my

Attorney!"

"Ok, have it your way."

Matts and Leeman stepped out in the hallway to discuss what to do with Mrs. Miller.

"You want to lock her up Henry?" Matts asked.

"No, we really don't have enough evidence just yet, let her go, we can't ask her any more questions without her lawyer. I would tell her not to leave town just to shake her up a little bit," Leeman said.

"Ok, Mrs. Miller, you are free to go, for now, don't leave town," Matts told Miller.

"Hey, fuck you, who the hell do you think you are telling me I can't leave town, you don't have anything on me or John, we didn't do anything wrong."

Matts shook his head as he left the room. Later that evening, he took a look at that file that Taylor faxed him. He notices in the medical report that a bite mark was found on one breast and buttocks. Matts had a strange feeling about this whole thing. He wanted to follow up with the investigation of the Kentucky case but thought at this point, the more he knew, the worse it would be on him. He noticed in Detective Taylors report that the car believed to be used in the killing was a blue Nineteen Sixty Nine GTO with Indiana plates. The report stated that the Bulish Police Department was currently looking for two men said to be white, with tattoos. The report stated that the plate from Indiana come back as stolen. Just as in the Clark County Case, the victim had marks of strangulation. Matts agreed with Taylor that the similarities between the two cases were no coincidence. To simply tear up the file so that Palmer didn't get his hands on it may be signing a death warrant on Millers wife. The only thing that didn't quite make sense was the eye witness testimony of Fran Keller who seen John Miller over by the body. How could somebody get something like that wrong, after all, she seen him with her own eyes. There's no way you could be standing around there and not see a dead naked girls body.

Chapter 7

The next morning, Sheriff Matts met with Sandra Davis, the young girl seen having sex with the Millers the night Chief Deputy Arlin Hants and Sheriff Matts went out to the Millers property.

"Please state your name for the record," Matts requested.

"My name is Sandy Davis."

"Now, Ms. Davis, as you may know, we are investigating the death of Abby Star. We know that you were at the Millers residence shortly after Abby Stars death, we also know that you were involved with the Millers in a sexual relationship, could you comment on that please?"

"Yes, I had a relationship with Kim Miller before her and John got together. I seen her at the Supermart earlier that afternoon, and, she asked me if I want to come over for drinks at her house."

"Was John drinking beer that night?"

"He did after he got home from work."

"What time did he get home from work?"

"I think it was about Six Thirty or so."

"Do you know where he was working that day?"

"At the Drug Store."

"How is it that you all come to having sex with each other?"

"We got really drunk, and, it just happened."

"Did John make the first moves on you?"

"No, he's too much of a square, we had to talk him into it, and he's not like that you know."

"When you say we, who do you mean?"

"Kim and I."

"Who made the first move?"

"Well, she and I kissed and...."

"She being Kim Miller?"

"Yes, and then I went over to John, and, just playing around, pulled his pants down, and started messing around with him."

"Did you use sex toys at all?"

"Yes, we used a vibrator and some crèmes, and stuff."

" Are you sure that John Miller didn't take advantage of you after he got you drunk, it may be hard to talk about, but, I need you to tell me the truth?"

"No, I made a move on him; he wasn't in to it really at all. I heard that he got upset about doing it the next day, but it was just innocent fun, you know, It was just a few drunk people acting stupid, like I said, he's too much of a square."

"Now, have you been back over there to have sex with them since that night?"

"No, I didn't go back over there because John was not feeling it, you know."

"Ok Ms. Davis, that's all I have for you, thanks for coming in."

Matts walked back to his office to call the Drug Store. He wanted to check out the story and see what time Miller got off of work that night. The owner of Lilly's Drug Store to Matts that he got off around Six Ten. Matts sunk back in his seat and started thinking about the information. If that prosecutor was not in such a rush to arrest Miller, he could have got this damn thing right.

Sheriff Matts went to see the County Attorney to find out what he should do to protect the Sheriff's Department and himself from possibly arresting an innocent man. It was also on his mind to see if he could reverse the injustice and get it right this time. He knew Leeman was never going to back down from the prosecution of Miller, like always, Leeman gets so caught up in the politics of a case, he loses sight of the proper objective, that is, to prosecute the right person for the right crime. Matts didn't understand why it was so hard for prosecutors to back off of a case when evidence comes to light of that they may be innocent. It was like, they see having to back down as a professional weakness or an incompetent practice of the law. They think the people who voted for them would think, huh, the prosecutor that we elected can't get a murder case right; he's just no good at being a prosecutor. What he should be thinking is I have made a bad mistake that will cost an innocent man his life, who cares if I am elected to the prosecutor's office again. Matts was not going out like that. He was elected to uphold the laws of the State and the constitution and thus, he is responsible to see that justice is served; even if that meant that he had to get the innocent freed. Matts owed the victim and the victim's family that much, they had the right to know who did this to their little girl, and to see that those responsible were prosecuted to the full extent of the law. Matts knew he would have a fight on his hands with Leeman. He also knew that this could cost him his position as Sheriff, but, he didn't care. An innocent man was in jail, and, killers were on the loose. Matts walked into the County Attorney's Office to speak to Raymond Gregg. He would know what to do.

"Come in Sheriff, you can go on in, Mr. Gregg is in his office."

"Thank you Sara," Matts replied.

"Hey John, what's on your mind?" Gregg asked Matts.

" I want to talk to you about the Abby Star case Ray, you see, information has come to my attention that the person arrested for this crime may in fact, be innocent. I received a call from a Detective Taylor of the Bulish Police Department, and, he has a case that factually matches our case. The suspects in that case were driving a car stolen from Albany and......"

" O boy, are you sure about this?"

"Yes, but Henry Leeman refuses to accept the fact that we have arrested the wrong man, he won't even hear me out."

"So, you're saying Leeman won't back off the case?"

"No, he won't, I need to do something here, what can I do?"

"Well, nothing really. You see John, it's your job to investigate a crime and then to turn your findings over to the Prosecutor who then decides that a prosecution should or should not take place. Thereafter, you simply become a witness for the State based on those findings. You as Sheriff have no further jurisdiction over the actual prosecution, that is only in the discretion of the prosecutor's office. The only standards under the law for the prosecutor are that he establishes probable cause that a crime was committed, and that, there is probable evidence that the accused committed the crime. As long as this has been accomplished, the prosecution can move forward."

"There has to be a way to stop it?"

"Now, let me stop you right there, be advised that Leeman can charge you with obstruction of justice and official misconduct. I suggest this. Write Leeman a letter explaining your conclusions as to your investigation. Be sure to include you belief in the innocence of the person arrested. Also, include the facts of the Bulisha case. This will protect you from Leemans reckless behavior.

"What about John Miller?"

"Hey, that's out of your hands. If I were you, I would continue to investigate the Kentucky case. You see, while Leeman is busy proving Millers guilt, you could be busy proving his innocence."

"That's it, that's what I will do, even though Leeman told me to destroy the Kentucky file so Gavin Palmer didn't get his hands on it."

"Wait just a minute, are you telling me that Leeman told you to destroy evidence that could prove Millers innocence?"

"Yes, he did."

"What the hell is this really all about John, there is more to this than meets the eye. It sounds like a political move to me. You get that letter together along with the attachments of the Bulisha file. Make sure you forward a copy of it all to me for the file, just in case we need it. Also, I want you to keep me informed about your findings on the Bulish Kentucky case. I always knew Leeman was a bad apple, but, to destroy evidence on a guy who is in jail facing the death penalty, wow, I mean, that's some rough stuff John, I'm shocked."

"You're shocked! you should be standing in my shoes."

"You know John, tampering with evidence is prosecutorial misconduct. He could be disbarred for that. As an Officer of the court, it may be my duty to report it to the State Bar Association."

"Well, I think you for your help Raymond."

"No problem let me know if I can be of anymore assistance."

Sheriff Matts headed back to his office to draft the letter and copy the Bulish file so he can attach the file to the letter. Matts was glad there was a way to do this without risking his position as Sheriff.

Letter to the Office of the Clark County Prosecutors Office;

Re: Abby Star, Case No. 8301-CCSD-221

From: Sheriff John Matts

Enclosed please find the Departments findings regarding the Star case. Also, please find attached the records of the Bulisha Police Department, Case No. 2236-83.

After careful consideration and upon completion of our investigation regarding this case, we find that both this case and the Bulisha Kentucky case have a relationship to each other requiring further investigation into the matter. We further find that this may lend evidence to the fact that John Miller, current defendant in the case, could be innocent of the pending charges and ask for you plenary consideration of the matter.

Best Regards,

Encl. Records, Bulisha P.D.   *Sheriff Jonathan Matts.*

Matts called Detective Taylor at the Bulisha Police Department to tell him he was coming down in the morning. Detective Matts welcomed Sheriff Matts and asked Matts to bring a copy of the Abby Star case with him.

Chapter 8

Later that night, John Miller set in cell at the Jail hoping someone would come and move him to a location with a phone. It was really hard setting in a cell day after day without getting some information from home about what was going on. A lot of people had come to the jail since he was arrested and they got moved to population within a day or so. He began to think they were just going to leave him there. The little five foot by five foot cell was driving him insane. If it did anything at all on a positive note, it gave him a chance to think about the situation. His mind raced to make sense of it all, but he failed to connect the dots. How they suspected that he had anything to do with this was all a mystery. He tried to think about classes he taught that Abby Star may have attended, but, couldn't remember any. He couldn't even remember her, much less a class he taught two years ago. No matter how many times he thought about the case, he always come back to the same reasoning, he knew he would be found innocent and set free, after all, he didn't do anything wrong, and, he had the best lawyer in the State to prove it.

"MILLER, GET YOUR STUFF, YOUR BEING MOVED!!!" a guard shouted into the tiny window of the cell.

"Thank god," Miller said as he gathered his stuff.

The guard escorted Miller back to cellblock "H". The huge green electric door made of bars opened slowly. Miller walked into the dayroom as the door slowly shut behind him. He walked back and put his bedding in one of the cell rooms within the cellblock. There were four bunks, two on each side, and a toilet in the middle. The cell room also had doors made of green bars. As he made his way back to the dayroom, he noticed in another cell room a blanket that was hanging to block anyone from seeing someone going to the bathroom. In the dayroom set a large metal picnic table facing a long set of green bars. Just on the other side of the bars was a TV that could not be reached by inmates. The cellblock was dirty and had an incredible smell, one that would take some getting used too. A look to the end of the dayroom revealed a payphone, or at least, what looked like a pay phone. There was an inmate on the phone and it appeared that he was going to be on there for a while.

Miller went over to the metal picnic table and took a seat on the end to wait for the phone to open.

"Hey, how's it going?" Miller said to another inmate seated on the end of the picnic table watching TV.

The other inmate looked at Miller with contempt and said, " Don't talk to me you baby rapper!" The inmate got up and walked back to a cell room. Miller looked away in shock acting as if he didn't hear that.

Miller noticed that the phone was open and walked over to make a phone call. He dialed home and got Kim.

"Hi babe, it's so good to hear from you, are you ok in there?"

"Yes, what's going on out there is somebody working on getting me out of here?"

"Mr. Palmer told your Dad that he was going to try and get you out on bond when you go to court, but, not to expect it. He said the Judge probably won't go for it."

"Well, they will let me out when they find out they made a

mistake," John said as he leaned against the dirty green wall.

"Mr. Palmer said that you will set in there for about a year before he can get the case to trial."

"A year, are you serious, I can't do this for a whole year, that just crazy!"

"Jonny, I want you to know that I love you very much. I miss you every minute of the day. I can't help but think this is all my fault. I know you didn't want to do that threesome and all. I just keep thinking about it."

"It's not your fault, it's just a mistake hunny, Palmer will get it all worked out, he's good Kim."

"I got a call from the school. They told me to come in and get your last check. I think they fired you from your job," Kim said as she started to cry.

"Imagine that, this is all a bad episode of the twilight zone. What if Palmer can't get me out of here, what if he can't get me out of this," John said as his heart began to race.

"This is all so hard to deal with John. I'm so worried about everything. They came and searched the house, took me in for questioning. I told them that I was not going to talk without a lawyer, and, they let me go."

"Good, don't talk to the bastards, next thing you know, they will be trying to arrest you."

"I get to visit you on visiting day; your mom won't talk to me anymore so I have to come up after she leaves. She thinks it's my entire fault."

"Don't worry about her, you know how she is, just keep cool, we will get out of this mess and move on with our life."

"YOU HAVE ONE MINUTE REMAING," a recording instructed.

"Well John, I love you, see you on visiting day."

John could hear Kim crying softly as to not let him know she was about to break down and loose it on the phone. "Its ok babe, it will all work out in the end, you'll see, it's just a little bit of time." Click, "YOUR TIME HAS EXPIRED."

John hung the phone up. He didn't even get to tell her he loved her. He walked away from the phone and headed back to the metal picnic table to watch some TV.

"Hey, come over here," an inmate said to John. John walked over to see what the inmate wanted. As he walked into the cell room, he could see two other inmates backed up in the corner.

"So, you like to fuck young girls huh?"

"What?" asked John as he looked to the guys behind him? Another inmate started swinging on him and three others joined in. One held his head down as the others continued to strike blows to his head and body. Blood began to splat across the dirty green walls. One inmate pulled his pants down and began to rape him. In all, six inmates took turns committing sexual acts on John Miller. They broke several bones and left him on the concrete floor in a pool of blood. He was face down and making sounds like he could not breathe. The inmates that were involved just walked over him and went to their cell rooms.

It was time for guards to make their rounds. As they walked around to cellblock "H", they noticed John Miller lying naked in the center of the floor.

"Everybody, get in your cells, NOW! Harry, we have an emergency back in cellblock "H", lock down the cells." Guards come back and entered the cellblock. One guard called to the dispatcher and had him summon for an ambulance. They waited for the EMT's before moving John.

The Jail Commander called Sheriff Matts at home to tell him what had happened. Matts told him to put John Miller in a single cell by himself when he returned from the hospital. Matts hung up the phone and shook his head.

"What's wrong babe?" Sara Matts said lying next to him in bed.

"It's a bad story getting worse by the minute Sara," Matts said as he turned over to her in bed. "It seems as though we got the wrong guy on the Star case. Now he's been beaten up and I guess raped in a cell at the jail."

"What does Henry Leeman say about it all John?"

"Nothing, he won't hear me out on it, I'm going to Bulisha Kentucky in the morning, we think the killers have done the same thing down there."

"You be careful down there John, do you think you can catch these guys?"

"I hope so, we are going to get something done to get this poor guy out of jail and get the real killers in."

John turned over to get some sleep.

At the hospital, the Emergency Department had to stop the bleeding and set Millers bones. They had to stich him up in three locations. They returned Miller back to the jail where a guard put him in a single cell as the Sheriff had ordered.

"Wow, what a night this has been," Guard Ralph Morgan said as he left the cell Miller was put in

"That's what the bastard gets for what he did." another guard said.

"For what he did, what did he do? it's my understanding that he has not been found guilty of anything yet." Morgan said with a puzzled look on his face.

"Like he didn't do it!" the guards said as they all began to laugh.

Chapter 9

He pulled himself up from the bed thinking about his long drive to Bulisha Kentucky. Matts didn't get much sleep; he tossed and turned most of the night. He could not get this case out of his mind. He knew he had to go down here and get this right. A man's life depended upon it, not to mention that there were killers somewhere running loose; no doubt, doing the same horrific acts over and over.

Matts got his shower and ate breakfast. He put the files together from the Abby Star case as well as the original file from the Bulisha Kentucky case. He also got the letter to the Prosecutor and the attached file along with a complete copy of both that would be forwarded to Ray Gregg. In addition to the letter and file to Ray Gregg, Matts included a notarized statement that reflected the conversation between Leeman and himself regarding Leemans order to tear up the file on Bulisha Kentucky. He headed out the door and ran over to the Post Office to mail it all off before he made his way south to Bulisha.

Five hours later, Sheriff Matts arrived in Bulisha. After looking for about an hour for the Bulisha Police Department, he made his way into the office and requested to see Detective Taylor.

"Sheriff Matts, it great to meet you," Taylor said as he came from an office at the end of the hallway.

"Likewise Detective," Matts replied. Matts put his hand in the air to return Taylors hand shake.

"Let me take you down to the crime lab, we should probably start there, Sheriff." Taylor and Matts took the steps down to a rather large crime lab.

"You have this much crime here in Bulisha?" Matts asked.

" Well, we are currently investigating three murders, two rapes, and two child abuse cases, that's an average week here in Bulisha," Answered Taylor as they walked into the lab.

"Wow, that seems to be a lot of crime for this little area," Matts said somewhat alarmed.

"Well, Bulisha County is not as small as it looks, there are one hundred thousand in the whole county, and down here, we have jurisdiction over the whole County even though were City Officers."

"That sounds like a system we need in Indiana, The Sheriff's Department has too many things to do, we have to serve papers for the court, run the County Jail, and patrol the entire County all at the same time."

"I trust your travels were ok, Sheriff?"

"Not too bad Detective, there's a lot of hills down here."

"Yes, we got a lot of hills, were actually known for our blue grass."

"I've not seen any blue grass, never the less; it's a beautiful country side."

"Thank you; it's where we call home."

Detective Taylor pulled out a file. "Here's the file on Macy Odem, she was seventeen at the time of her death."

Taylor opened the file to reveal a copy of a diploma from North Bulisha High School. The next item was a picture of the crime scene including the body of Odem. Matts noticed the bite marks and opened the Star file to compare the marks. "Now, here are the photos of Abby Star, as you can see Detective, these bite marks appear to be from the same person."

A plastic bag revealing a black hair was in the evidence box.

Matts could see that it was close to the hair found at the Star scene.

"What have you found out so far Detective?"

"Well, we know that Odem was picked up by two men driving a blue nineteen sixty-nine GTO with Indiana plates. Our Medical Examiner has concluded that Macy died due to a loss of blood." Taylor turned the pages of the file back to the crime scene picture. "As you can see here from the picture, both lower areas of the body were torn due to excessive sexual intercourse. The M.E. believes that Macy endured several hours of sexual intercourse, even a few hours past her death."

"You mean they raped her after she was dead?" Matts asked with a shocking look to his face.

"No, they just never stopped!" Taylor replied.

"That's just crazy," Matts said as he looked at the picture. "Who could be so inhuman, just animals!"

"Well, we have an APB out on the car, so we hope to find out the answer to that very soon," Taylor replied.

"These cases are identical, there's no doubt these crimes were committed by the same people, now, and it's just a matter of finding these monsters." Matts concluded.

"We need to find them as soon as possible, they could be doing this again as we speak." Taylor said as he slammed the file on the lab table.

"No doubt, we are dealing with serial killers here. I would not be surprised to find a path of crime from these lowlifes," Matts said.

"Yeah, I have been comparing cases with three other departments," Taylor instructed.

"What do they have," Matts asked.

"I'm waiting on those files now, all the evidence tends to show that the suspects are located here, but, we have not found the car yet. An officer from the County Department got word from someone last night that the sixty nine GTO was seen heading out Kentucky nine. We have officers out there checking the area now."

"Great, sure love to help catch those freaks while I'm down here." Matts said as he continued looking through the file.

A cop ran into the lab obviously excited. "We found the GTO, its out off of Kentucky nine." Matts and Taylor jumped up from their seats.

"Don't do anything until we get there!" They started for the door. "Come on Sheriff, looks like you may get your wish."

Matts and Taylor ran out to Taylors SUV. As they drove out Kentucky nine, Matts pulled his service revolver and made sure it was loaded. They pulled up to the small country hide out and seen the sixty nine GTO setting in the driveway. They got out and drew their service revolvers as they slowly approached the front door. Matts and Taylor stopped short behind the GTO and bent down. They set their service revolvers to cover the Officers who were about to kick the door in. Taylor waived the Officers in. Suddenly, shots were fired coming from inside the house. Taylor ran around the GTO and proceeded to charge his way into the front door. Matts saw out of the corner of his eye one of the suspects running off towards the woods in the back of the house. Matts ran after the suspect shouting, " Stop or be shot". The suspect turned and fired a shot at Matts and kept running. Matts aimed his weapon and fired one shot at the suspect. The suspect dropped to the ground. Matts ran up to the suspect and bent down to check his pulse. He was dead. As he started to get up, he heard behind him, "YOU KILLED MY BROTHER, YOU SON OF A BITCH!" The second suspect started firing at Matts. Matts was able to get one shot off towards the second suspect. The second suspect aimed his weapon at Matts head and fired a shot. Matts dropped to the ground.

Taylor came running out of the back door and fired a shot at the second suspect killing him instantly. He walked over to Matts and bent down. Matts was dead.

Taylor dropped to the ground next to Matts and held his hand. Taylor just set there looking at Matts still holding his service revolver in his hand. Another Officer came over to Taylor and bent down to help him up. "Let me help you up Detective, he's gone Sir, he's gone."

"You just let me lone now, you hear, you let me lone."

The other Officers stood up and stopped what they were doing. They looked over to Taylor and watched him hold Matts hand. Taylor put his hand to his mouth and began to weep. After all the noise from the shots fired, and the rush from the incident, all you could hear was the wind slowly blowing by, and, the soft sounds of Taylors weeping into the open air.

Taylor got up from the ground and went into the house to search for evidence. Taylor found a bag in the bedroom containing rope, masking tape, and several video tapes. Other Officers found ID's on both the dead suspects and ran them for warrants. Taylor called for the Medical Examiner and a tow truck to impound the GTO.

Later at the Bulisha Police Department, Detective Taylor set the evidence he had collected in an evidence room and called for a VCR to review the tapes. He was in hopes that he could find evidence of the rapes for both Odem and Star. The Bulisha Crime Lab was still at the little house on Kentucky Nine collecting blood samples and other evidence.

" We have a return on the ID's Detective Taylor," an Officer said as he entered the room." Alvin Hatcher, 150 N. State Road Nine, Bulisha Kentucky and Marvin D. Hatcher, 332 First St, Albany Indiana. Alvin Hatcher is on parole for rape and Marvin Hatcher has a warrant out of Indiana for armed robbery and is wanted for questioning in the State of Ohio for the disappearance of a female college student." The Officer handed Detective Taylor a file on the Hatchers.

"Imagine that!" Detective Taylor said as he opened the file. "Call up to Ohio and get a picture of the missing girl so I can see if she's on these tapes."

He put one of the tapes in, and, just as he thought, it was a rape scene. Taylor watched as the Hatchers Brothers raped an unknown female. He started to feel sick as the tape went on. He could hear the female begging for them to stop. They just kept going as if they never heard anything. Detective Taylor pulled the file of Abby Star and placed the picture next to the TV screen to help identify in case she was on one of these horrific tapes. He looked down and counted twenty two tapes. Suddenly it hit him that he was about to reveal twenty two different rapes. How many of these girls, he wondered, would be dead. After quickly going through all the tapes, he did not identify Abby Star, but, did find the rape scene of Macy Odem.

Chapter 10

May Third, Nineteen Eighty Three, the Clark Daily Record;

CLARK COUNTY SHERIFF SHOT DEAD IN KENTUCKY SHOOTOUT.

The Daily Record has just learned that Sheriff John Matts was killed in a shootout in Bulisha Kentucky. It is unknown at this time what Sheriff Matts was investigating or why he was involved in a gun battle in the State of Kentucky. Sources tell the Daily Record that Matts and a Detective from Bulisha were in pursuit of two men when one of the men fired a shot at Matts. Matts returned fire killing that suspect but was shot from behind by a second suspect. Records of the incident are currently being sealed as the FBI has been called in to investigate.

County Attorney Ray Gregg slowly lowered the newspaper and set it on his desk.

Gregg's secretary came into his office holding a package in her hand. "Sorry to bother you Ray, you got this package in the mail this morning."

"That's ok Sara, thank you."

Gregg opened the package to find Sheriff Matts letter and the file. He looked over the file and the notarized statement from Matts regarding the conversations between Leeman and Matts about destroying evidence. Gregg got on the phone and called Gavin Palmers office.

"Gavin, this is Ray Gregg, how are you today?"

"Fine Ray, what can I do for you?"

"Doing ok, I was wondering if I could come over to your office, I need to speak to you about the Abby Star case?"

"Yes, I have to be in court at one this afternoon, if you could come over now?"

"I am on my way Gavin!"

"Thanks see you in a bit," Palmer said as he hung the phone up.

Gregg gathered the file and letter and headed out the door.

"Come on in Ray," Palmer said standing in the doorway to his office. "Would you care for a cup of java?"

"That would be great Gavin. Thank you." Gregg replied as he set the large file down at the edge of Palmers desk.

"What's on your mind Ray?"

"Well Gavin, I had a meeting a few days ago with Sheriff Matts and he expressed some concern about the Star case to me. You see, he believed that your client is innocent but could not get Leeman to drop the case against him. Leeman ordered Matts to destroy this file so that you didn't get your hands on it." Gregg reached over and handed Palmer the file.

"Now, you see Gavin, he sent me this file because he believes that these are the real killers and that they have committed the crimes in Kentucky as well. In fact, Matts lost his life attempting to prove it."

"Yes Ray, I seen that in the paper this morning," Palmer said as he opened the file. "What's this?" Palmer asked as he held up the affidavit.

"It's an affidavit from Matts about Leemans orders to destroy the file."

"Who is Detective Taylor?"

"I believe he is the Detective on the Bulisha Kentucky case," Gregg said pointing to a Bulisha Police report.

"Sara, call over to the courthouse and get the Smith case continued, I am going to Bulisha Kentucky." Palmer instructed.

"I hope that helps you out Gavin," Gregg said as he held his hand out for a shake.

Palmer shook Gregg's hand. "Well, I can't thank you enough Ray, good work. I will see that the Supreme Court and the Bar Association gets a copy of this affidavit. That will get Leeman just what he deserves."

Palmer left Clark County for Bulisha Kentucky. He met with Detective Taylor who seemed very happy to see him." I'm so glad to meet you Mr. Palmer, when Sheriff Matts got killed; it left me with the thought that the case of Abby Star was incomplete. There was still an innocent man in jail and a good cop lost his life attempting to prove it," Taylor told Palmer with obvious emotion.

"I thank you for that Detective; I intend to set the record straight on that!" Palmer assured Taylor.

"Let's take a ride out Kentucky Nine, were the Hatchers stayed," Taylor said as they walked out of the station.

The two arrived at the Hatchers hide-out. "Here's where your Sheriff was shot, Mr. Palmer," Taylor said pointing to a blood spot in the dirt.

"Well, I have to respect the fact that Matts went way beyond his duty to do what was right. He was one in a million."

"We found the evidence in here. It contained twenty-two rape tapes of which we are still trying to identify the girls in them. Taylor said pointing to the bedroom.

"If you could be so kind Detective Taylor, I would like a sample of these blood splats. I am in hopes that I may need to compare these blood types to the blood samples found at the Abby Star scene."

"I have had all the evidence, including the rape tapes, copied for you to take with you. Among them, you have a report and the actual physical samples."

"Great, you're on this Detective," Palmer said in observance. "I was wondering if you would testify in court should this go to trial."

"Yeah, I'm there, just name the time." Taylor opened a file and pointed to a report from the Bulisha County Medical Examiner's Office. "I am having the blood samples we found in the trunk of the Hatchers car checked. I am in hopes that we can get a match on Abby Star. That would go a long way in proving that your client didn't do the crimes he charged with."

"Good idea, call me when you find out the results Detective."

Palmer gathered up the box of evidence and headed back to Clark County. He spent the rest of the night drawing up a motion to have Henry Leeman removed from the case for prosecutorial misconduct. The motion cited Leemans intent to withhold material evidence from the defense. The motion also cited the fact that a complaint having been filed before the State Bar, the prejudicial effect of having the behavior of Leeman reviewed would create an situation of conflict that would be so unfair to the defendant as to prevent him from receiving a fair trial, simply put, that Leeman should step down as a matter of law.

The Next morning, Palmer shot over to the courthouse and filed his motion in the Clerk's Office. As Palmer was leaving, he heard the Clerk calling him.

"The Judge needs to see you Gavin," the Clerk stated.

"Very well then!" Palmer replied.

Palmer walked around the counter and headed back to the Judges Office. "Judge Thomas, what can I do for you?" Palmer asked.

"Gavin, have you lost your mind?" Judge Thomas asked as he reviewed the papers. "What are you thinking filing a motion like this?"

"It is what it is Judge!"

"Ok then, I will set this motion for hearing at one this afternoon!" Judge Thomas said without delay.

"See you then Judge," Palmer said as he walked out the door.

One that afternoon, Clark Superior Court;

"Comes now the defendant, by counsel, and moves the court to consider a motion to have the Prosecutor, Henry Leeman, removed from the case in State of Indiana vs. John Miller. Show The State present by Henry Leeman, the defendant present by counsel, Gavin Palmer. Court considers the motion and finds that this court lacks jurisdiction to hear this action. I find that the sole jurisdiction to hear Attorney misconduct matters are in the State Supreme Court and as such, your motion is denied Mr. Palmer. Now, I am going to set this case for priority jury trial and I will have the date moved up....."

Palmer jumped up," Objection your honor, there is no reason to move the case up, we are working on evidence that will take some time to process,"

"You have had five months to get this case together Mr. Palmer, now, this case was originally set for November twenty second if I'm correct," Judge Thomas said looking to the court staff for conformation

"You are just moving this case up because you know it will only take the State Bar three months to hear the Attorney misconduct matter. Palmer shouted as he pointed his finger to the Judge. "You are violating my clients Sixth Amendment right to a fair trial."

"MR. PALMER," yelled the Judge, you had better watch what you say to me, you could find yourself in contempt, now........."

"FINE MYSELF IN CONTEMPT! you set this trial for priority, I will have you all thrown off this case," Palmer shouted as he walked around the table approaching the Judge. "This is a murder trial; the defense has a right under the Fourteenth Amendment of the United States Constitution to due process. We have the right to prepare a defense and not be subjected to political games between to butt buddies.........."

" THATS IT PALMER, you are now in contempt of court, one more word out of you and you will wake up in the County Jail!, now, the Sixth Amendment calls for a fast and speedy trial. The trial will be set on the Tenth of June, jury selection to begin........."

Palmer got up and stormed out of the court room. SLAM, sounded the doors as Palmer left. Judge Thomas and Henry Leeman jumped in reaction

"Jury selection is to begin on June Ninth at Eight am." Judge Thomas finished saying after watching Palmer leave in the middle of his sentence.

Chapter 11

"Nice entrance there Detective, sort of figured you'd be showing up," Palmer said in excitement. "You know, I'm not putting you on the stand until the State rests its case, about two days or so," Palmer instructed.

"Well, I figured you could use a good investigator, and since I'm the best I know."

The two men laughed. "Good man Taylor, come on in and I will fix us a drank," The trial of John Miller was going to start tomorrow, the town was talking and the news organizations were filling up the hotel rooms. As you went up to the court room you could see a reporter outside in the courtyard giving his report on the upcoming trial. Inside the court of Judge Thomas, you could see people scrambling in and out of the room as jury selection was about an hour from starting.

Palmer was about to leave home for the courthouse. He decided to stop by the coffee shop and get a large coffee before heading over for jury selection. As he walked in, he noticed people looking at him with a strange stare. He went up to the counter and ordered one black coffee, no sugar or dairy to go. The waitress, without saying anything to him, walked over and began pouring his coffee. It was a very unusual mood in the coffee shop and Palmer knew it had everything to do with the trial of John Miller. He knew that he just interrupted an ongoing conversation about John Miller and the trial, and he also knew that already, people were taking the opposite opinion to his client. Palmer shook his head with a bit of a smile and started for the door. It was not unusual to see people acting like that, Palmer knew from experience that once a person is arrested for a crime like this, they are guilty and the lawyer that defends him is a piece of shit. It was just another day in the life of a criminal defense lawyer.

Later as Palmer entered the courtroom, he could see Leeman's huge staff running around like headless chickens. The courtroom was packed with people as far as the eye could see. Palmer knew that he was going to have to pick a jury from this crowd.

"Good morning Gavin", said the court reporter.

"Good morning Irene, you know, you are the first person to say that to me today!"

"Well, that's the profession you chose Gavin"

"Indeed it is", Palmer said as he set at the defense table.

"ALL RISE, the Superior Court in and for the 26th Judicial Circuit is now in session, the Honorable Judge Thomas presiding" Judge Thomas came out and set at the bench.

"State of Indiana v. John Miller, show the State present by Henry Leeman, Prosecuting Attorney, the Defendant John Miller present in person and by Counsel, Gavin Palmer. Defendant is in the custody of the Clark County Sheriff, ok...we are here for the purpose of jury selection today...are there any pre-trial motions that need to be heard before trial begins in the morning counsel?", asked the Judge.

"Nothing from me your Honor," Leeman answered.

"The defense would like to show an objection on the record for the violation of the defendants 6th amendment right to prepare a defense given the limited amount of time he has had to do so," Palmer instructed.

"Your objection is noted, can we please move on," Judge Thomas suggested with a not so bright look on his face. "Please bring in the first 15 prospective jurors," the Judge ordered.

Palmer looked over to John Miller; he could see that John was an emotional wreck. " You're going to be ok son, just take it easy, I will win this, you have got to trust me, I give you my word," Palmer said as he looked over to Leeman with contempt. After 8 hours of questions to prospective jurors, they finally had a jury.

Palmer headed out of the courtroom. He had to prepare the case for trial and he knew Leeman would come at him hard first thing in the morning. It was getting dark as Palmer pulled up to his office. As he went to put a key in the front door, Palmer heard the sound of footsteps.

"Well counselor, you ready to get this done?" a voice said from nowhere. Palmer turned around, "who's there?"

A figure came towards him from the dark.

"Did you think I could just set at home and let you fight this without any help?"

Palmer noticed it was Detective Taylor.

Chapter 12

Day One, State v. John Miller.

Palmer pulled up in his old car ready for the first day of trial. The press was everywhere as they had been the day before. It was as if they never left. He noticed some of the reporters heading over to his car to get that great pretrial statement from the defense and any predictions Palmer may make regarding the outcome.

"Mr. Palmer, could you comment on this trial, is your client innocent?" asked a Reporter.

"It would be inappropriate for me to do that. You want to know what the facts of this case are, come watch the trial. That is what trials are for, to establish the facts. You want a prediction on the outcome? Get yourself a crystal ball," Palmer said as he gathered his things for trial.

Palmer walked in and placed two boxes of paperwork on the defense table. From the side door, he saw John Miller being brought in via the Sheriff's Department. The Judge was set at the door waiting to be announced by the Court Bailiff. Palmer turned his head to look at the crowd behind him. He noticed Detective Taylor giving him thumbs up. On the other side was County Attorney Ray Gregg who gave Palmer a nod.

The Bailiff walked up to the front of the courtroom;

"ALL RISE, Court will now come to order, the Superior Court in and for the 29th Judicial Circuit is now in session, the Honorable Judge Thomas is presiding," the Bailiff instructed as she walked away. Judge Thomas walked in and took his seat at the bench.

"State of Indiana v John Miller, show the State present by Mr. Leeman, show the Defendant present in person and by Counsel, Mr. Palmer, show also that the defendant appears in the custody of the Sheriff's Department as per this court's order….now, are we ready to proceed Counselor's?"

"We are ready to go Judge," Leeman answered.

"Let's do this," Palmer instructed.

Judge Thomas looked at Palmer with a questionable look. "We are on for trial, if there be nothing further, please bring in the Jury,"

Judge Thomas instructed.

The Bailiff went into the Jury room and had them take their seats in the jury box. After a great deal of instructions to the jury from the Judge, the trial began.

"You may call your first witness, Mr. Prosecutor," instructed the Judge.

"State call's Dale Row to the stand," instructed Leeman.

"Mr. Row, could you state your name and tell the jury where you are employed?"

"My name is Dale Row and I am a bartender at the Fox Club."

"Mr. Row, were you on duty or at work on the night of January 25th of this year?"

"Now, did you see the defendant that night in the bar and if so, what were the times, that is, what time did you see him enter and then leave?"

"I saw John come in about 9:30 or so and he left about 11:00 pm… and I'm not exactly sure what time he left, I was pretty busy that night."

"Now, can you tell the jury how he acted around you?"

"OBJECTION, is the State actually asking this witness to testify as to the defendants state of mind?" Palmer shouted.

"Sustained, please move on Mr. Leeman," ordered the Judge.

"No further questions you're Honor," instructed Leeman.

"Your witness Mr. Palmer," said the Judge.

"Thank you you're Honor, Mr. Row, did you see Abby Star with the defendant at any time that night or in your life?"

"No."

"Did you see the defendant kill Abby Star?"

"No Sir"

"Nothing further of this witness," Palmer said as he returned to his seat.

"Mr. Prosecutor?" said the Judge.

"I have no additional questions for Mr. Row; State calls Dale Moss to the stand."

"Given the fact that we had a late start, we will break for lunch and then you can call your next witness at that time Mr. Leeman," instructed the Judge.

After lunch, the State called Dale Moss who testified that he discovered the body of Abby Star near the trash dumpster, half naked and full of blood. He thin called Coroner Robert Johnson who testified that the victim died from an excessive loss of blood. Johnson testified that there were also signs of strangulation. He testified that there indeed was a rape, however could not confirm that it was a gang rape on cross-examination, nor could he completely rule it out. The State admitted hair samples found on the body and hinted to the jury that the hair was the same as the defendants. On cross examination, the Coroner admitted that millions of people had the same hair. The Coroner testified that Abby Star had been drugged and had the smell of beer on her body but none was found in her blood

The Judge ended the proceedings for the day. Palmer gathered his things and left the courthouse to get prepared for day 2.

Chapter 13

Day Two; State v John Miller

The Judge stepped in the courtroom to make sure all the parties to the trial were present and ready to go. Palmer was at the defense table looking over a file. The Prosecutor was not at his table, but many of his staff were there setting numerous exhibits on the states table in preparation for the day.

The Bailiff called the court to order and Judge Thomas took the bench.

"Mr. Prosecutor, your next witness, Sir," instructed the Judge.

"Thank you your Honor, State calls as its next witness...Fran Keller."

Fran Keller got up and walked over to the witness stand.

"Take a seat there Ms. Keller," Leeman instructed. "Now, were you at the Fox Club on the night in question?"

"I was."

"And did you see the defendant on the property at that time?"

"I did."

"How do you know it was the defendant?"

"He was standing out back by the dumpster acting very strange."

"OBJECTION, MOVE TO STRIKE, witness cannot possibly testify as to the way the defendant *acted*, she is not a psychologist or an expert witness," Palmer stated.

"OVERRULED, the witness can testify as to the demeanor of the defendant in the commission of a crime," Judge Thomas ordered.

"COMMISSION OF........ARE YOU OUT OF YOUR MIND! The witness must establish if it is her opinion or fact......," Palmer shouted in grave disagreement.

"Your objection is noted, now let's move on Mr. Palmer," the

Judge ordered.

"Ok Ms. Keller, tell the court, where was the defendant standing when you saw him?" asked Leeman.

"Right where the body of Abby Star was found!"

Palmer's face turn three shades of blue. He could see the reaction of the jury as they looked at each other in amazement.

"How do you know that a body was later located at that very spot?"

"I explained it to the police that I saw him standing right there, where the body was."

"No further questions, your witness," Leeman stated.

Palmer smiled at Ms. Keller; He got up and started walking towards the witness.

"Ms. Keller, did you see the defendant raping or killing Abby Star?"

"No, I did not!"

"No further questions, defense moves to strike the testimony of this witness in reference to how the defendant acted, she has just testified that she did not see the defendant engaged in the commission of a crime," Palmer said looking to Leeman with a smile.

"Sustained, the jury will disregard the testimony of this witness as it relates to the way the defendant acted, Mr. Prosecutor, your next witness please."

"State calls Arlin Hants to the stand."

"Please state your name and rank for the record please," Leeman instructed.

"My name is Arlin Hants; I am Chief Deputy with the Clark County Sheriff's Department."

"Deputy Hants, were you in fact the lead investigator in the Abby Star case?"

"Along with Sheriff Matt's, yes."

"Now, as part of your investigation, did you review the body of

Abby Star, and how did your investigation lead to the defendant in this case."

"I did review the body and noticed a smell of alcohol on her. I further noticed a black hair fitting the defendants......"

"OBJECTION, witness is testifying in narrative," Palmer said.

"OVERRULED, the witness can testify in narrative," the Judge ordered.

"Any way's, I interviewed Ms. Keller who saw the defendant at the scene of the crime so I went out to Mr. Millers and..."

"What did you see Deputy?" Leeman interrupted.

"I saw the defendant and his wife having sex with a young girl, there were beer cans everywhere."

"Did you later identify the young girl?"

"It was a girl by the name of Davis; she was in the defendant's class one year earlier."

"Do you know if Abby Star was a student of the defendants?"

"Yes, she was in the same class." The courtroom erupted.

"Order, bring it down or find yourself in contempt of this court," the Judge ordered.

"Thank you Deputy, no further questions," Leeman said taking a seat at the States table.

"Mr. Palmer?" the Judge instructed.

"Deputy Hants, do you now, or, have you ever had any physical evidence linking the defendant to this crime?" Palmer asked on cross.

"Only circumstantial evid..."

"I simply asked you for a yes or no, you do or you don't!" Palmer interrupted.

"No, I do not."

"Did you witness the defendant in the alleged act?

"No, of course not."

"No further questions," Palmer said taking his seat.

The State presented 3 more hours of testimony before resting its case. Palmer looked at John Miller and assured him that the case was as good as won. He got up and headed for the door.

Chapter 14

Palmer headed across town to his office. He knew he had to go over a lot of evidence if he intended to offer it at trial. It was sure to be a long night. Palmer knew that he had to get the evidence of the Hatchers to the jury. It was not going to be easy given the fact that the Hatchers were dead. He does not have any confessions or statements from them, he has no physical evidence to present to the jury pointing the finger at the Hatchers, and, he has no Sheriff Matts to testify regarding his extended investigation. All he really had at this point was a group of crimes committed by Marvin and Alvin Hatcher that factually matched the Abby Star case. It would be Leemans argument at trial that, if one were to look hard enough, they could find thousands of cases that factually matched the Abby Star case. It was indeed necessary to place these thugs at the crime scene. To somehow show a path of rape and murder that touched the life of Abby Star, even if it related to them being seen getting a hamburger together. It was clear that there had to be proof offered in court that the Hatchers at least knew Abby Star. Otherwise, it's just a simple theory. Somebody had to see these guys together somewhere. It's hard to believe that two boys can pick up a young girl and not be seen by somebody somewhere.

Palmer called over to Detective Taylors hotel room and asked him to come over to his office so they could discuss the case in further detail. He pulled the file containing the evidence in the Bulisha Kentucky case. He pulled the pictures of Abby Star and compared them to the pictures of Macy Odem. It was clear that the bite marks on the two girls were an exact match. Reports from the Medical Examiners matched as well. Strangulation and the cause of death, a loss of blood due to excessive sexual intercourse. Palmer knew that the jury would see this evidence and come to the same conclusion that he had. As a defense lawyer, it should only be necessary to show the jury that there was a good possibility that these crimes were committed by somebody else. It should only be necessary to establish a reasonable doubt that Miller committed the crime. Palmer noticed a report listing an address for one of the Hatcher brothers in Albany Indiana.

"Palmer, you here?" Detective Taylor called out.

"Come on in Detective, I'm back here in my office," Palmer replied.

"I see you are working hard over here Gavin," Taylor said looking around the room at all the files and evidence scattered about. "Great job in court today, boy that was really something. I know who to call if I ever need a criminal lawyer!" Taylor said with excitement.

"Let's hope you never need one Detective."

"Well, you never know in the world we live in today."

"Do I ever know how true that is, have a seat Detective, I'm just going over all this evidence. Say, have you ever been to this Albany Indiana address?" Palmer asked pointing to a police report.

"No, the case ended for us when those boys were killed. We had enough evidence on them to close the case," Taylor replied.

"Are you up for a little field trip tonight Detective Taylor?" Palmer asked with a grin.

"You know, I thought you would never ask. Nothing like a little detective work."

The men got in Palmers old Chrysler and headed up the road for Albany.

"I will tell you what I am looking for Detective; I need to place the Hatchers at the scene of the crime. The evidence between the two cases is clear and speaks volumes; however, if I can't show some kind of contact, it's just a matter of speculation. I need to connect the physical evidence in the Star case to the Hatchers," Palmer said driving extremely fast up the road in that big car.

"Right, I got you," Taylor said holding on to the dash.

"Somewhere, somebody had to see these guys around here on the night of Stars death. I am hoping that we can find somebody who remembers seeing Abby Star around those boys, or better yet, with them. That simple little fact alone, with the other evidence, would ensure a not-guilty verdict in this case. Without that, it is just an unproven theory of the defense."

Taylor had both hands on the dash; it seemed the more Palmer talked about the case, the faster he went." Yeah, I see your point there Gavin."

"It's really like this, the jury may believe it, or, they may not. A jury wants to know what happened, it's a matter of assigning blame. It's not enough to find that John Miller didn't do it without knowing who did. In the absence of establishing who did it, most juries will see one-sided and convict, if for no other reason but to make sure that they serve justice by eliminating any possibility that the second they set a person free for a lack of evidence, they offend again."

Palmer was reaching speeds of ninety miles an hour. Taylor was looking out the side window watching the trees past by very quickly. You could hear a tremble in his response." Yeah, uh huh."

"It's been my experience that the jury looks past the fact that the State didn't have their shit together in time for trial as fare as the evidence is concerned, the Prosecutor has an advantage in that he represents the people of the State, and, jurors are people of the State. Essentially, the Prosecutor represents the jury. He is their Attorney as well. In addition, Prosecutors are viewed as having been god-sent, whereas, defense attorneys are nothing more than slick con-artist trying to get dirt bag off so he can go and commit more crimes. Having said that, as long as the State presents enough evidence to show a reasonable possibility that the defendant could have did it, they do what they believe is best and convict."

"I'm feeling lightheaded, did you want me to drive while you talk, or, possibly go over the paperwork in the files Gavin?"

"Nah, that's ok, we are almost there." Palmer said shooting down the two lane road. "It really is a high stakes gamble Detective, its nothing less than a game of craps. The law says a person should be found not-guilty if there is a reasonable doubt as to his guilt, when in reality, it should say that he be found not guilty if there is *any* doubt whatsoever. After all, what is reasonable to one may be entirely different to another."

"I see what you're saying, that's only seems fair. That seems to make the standard of innocent until proven guilty somewhat of a sham," Taylor replied.

"In deed it does, you see, most defendants who are charged with a crime are guilty in most people's minds the minute they are arrested. They are seen in hand cuffs being carried off to jail by the police and appear guilty because of the arrest scene itself. Most people believe that they are guilty just for the simple fact that they wouldn't be getting arrested if they didn't do something wrong. That would just be un-American. It really has to overcome an unofficial standard that the defendant is guilty until he can prove by clear evidence otherwise. Still then, many people believe that they are guilty; they just found a way to get off. That's why I become a defense attorney rather than a prosecutor or a judge. Somebody has to step up and be there for innocent people or the great system of American criminal jurisprudence is reduced to a one-sided mythical existence of ideas of justice based on questionable facts and a prosecutor's subjective beliefs and creative imagination. Take this case for instance, Leeman presented a whole bunch of evidence and put on this big show in front of the jury, made the facts appear so damn incriminating, yet, you and I both know, as did Sheriff Matts, that Miller is completely innocent. It was nothing more than a magic act. The crazy thing is, a lot of prosecutors do this, and it's just part of their M.O. That may seem unfair, but the truth is, the American Criminal Jury Trial is nothing more than planned theatrics. If you're looking for the truth, the last place you will find it is in a courtroom."

"Your right, that's pretty wise, I never thought it out like that," Taylor said thanking god they were finally there.

They pulled up to the front of the house and walked up to the front door. They knocked a few times and waited for an answer. A young girl answered.

"Yes?"

"Hello, my name is Gavin Palmer, and........"

"I know who you are, what do you want?"

"We are attempting to locate any information on Marvin and Alvin Hatcher that we can."

"There dead."

"Yes, but, are you a family member?"

"I am their little Sister!"

"May we come in and talk with you?"

"About what?"

"Well, we have a few questions about your brothers."

"I guess so." They walked into the small house and had a seat on the couch.

"Do your parents live here?"

"No, we were adopted as kids."

"Did your brothers live here?"

"Alvin did, Marvin lived in Kentucky."

"Do you know a girl named Abby Star?"

"The girl that was killed, I knew who she was."

"Did you ever hang out with her?"

"A few times."

"Did she ever hang out here?"

"A few times, you think my brothers killed her don't you."

"Why do you say that?" Taylor asked.

"I can just tell."

"Did your brother ever hang out with her?"

"Nope."

"He didn't know her at all?"

"Nope."

"When she was here hanging out with you, was your brother ever here?"

"No."

"Would you mind if we looked in his room?"

"I am late for work; you can come back another time."

"Ok, we will do that, thank you for your time."

She walked them to the door and didn't say anything as they left.

"She's a liar," Taylor said to Palmer.

"Yeah, she's not telling the truth.

"Let's drive around the block and see if she really goes to work," Taylor suggested.

They drove around the corner and waited. About ten minutes later they seen her walk out her back door with a large black garbage bag and toss it in the trash can. After about an hour, she finally left.

Palmer started the car and headed down the alley to see what was in the bag. Taylor jumped out and pulled the bag open.

"Bingo," Taylor said, " it's full of naked pictures and shit." He tossed the bag in the car and they took off for Clark County.

Back at the office, Taylor pulled out several pictures of the Hatchers lying naked on their backs.

"What is the deal with these freaks," Taylor said to Palmer.

"I don't know," replied Palmer, "the problem is that there are no pictures of Abby Star."

"I will run back up there in the morning to see what I can find out, somebody knows something. Maybe if I tell her that we saw her tossing this shit in the trash, she will tell me more about the situation."

"Good idea let me know what you find out. I will see you after court." Palmer said as Taylor left.

Chapter 15

Day Three, Jury Trial of John Miller.

Palmer walked in the courtroom and set his files on the defense table. It was going to be another great day of litigation in the American Legal System. As he took his seat at the table, he noticed the Judge at the bench having a conversation with Henry Leeman. That was not unusual, but, it did call for Palmer's attention. It is unethical for the judge to discuss a case with the Prosecutor, without opposing counsel present. If Palmer made a big deal of it, they would just say they were talking about an upcoming golf match at the Local Bar Association.

Palmer knew that Judge Thomas and Henry Leeman were old friends. They went to Law School together and Leeman, like most lawyers in this town, was always sucking up to the Judge. You can tell which of the lawyers were brown noses. They played politics to get an advantage in the courtroom. You can always see them right up there chewing the fat with the Judge. Sometimes, it's so funny to watch them stand up there and try to come up with something to talk about; they will lower their head in an attempt to think of something more to say. It's almost part of the daily procedure, *"well, got to get up here and think of something funny to say to the Judge to get him on my side today."* My take on it, the lawyer that has to suck up to the Judge in an attempt to get a good outcome on his case, knows he is not much of a lawyer. Like a scared child, he needs the Judge to hold his hand through the cases he litigates. The problem with most lawyers these days is that they are participating members of the same club. In my opinion, that does their clients a huge disservice. It works great for the client that gets a good deal because their lawyer is good friends with the prosecutor, but, where a favor was extended in one case; a favor is expected to be returned in another. It's a give and take situation. *"You scratch my back, I will scratch yours."* The lawyer will take a case that has little chance of winning, or, a client that he don't give a damn about, and make a deal with the Prosecutor to even the score for the last favor he got. The lawyer will then turn around and tell their client that he has to take a deal because there is no way of winning it at trial, and if he doesn't, he will get a lot more time out of it. You would be better off hiring the Prosecutor to represent you and prosecute at the same time. At least you would have someone on your side. A real lawyer will take that case that has little chance of winning, and win it!

Leeman walked back to his table and reached in his briefcase to pull out some papers. He walked over to Palmer and set the papers down in front of him. Without saying anything, he just walked away. Palmer shook his head and reached for the papers. It was a *Motion in Limine.* A motion in limine is a motion a lawyer files in an attempt to exclude evidence that he believes the other lawyer plans to present to the jury. It is a motion that ask the Judge to rule that the evidence expected to be presented by the defense has no basis in the law and that it will only serve to confuse the jury. In this case, Leeman is asking the Judge to exclude any and all evidence regarding Detective Taylor, the Hatcher boys, or, any crimes committed by the Hatchers. It is an attempt to deny John Miller his constitutionally protected right to a fair trial and to present to the jury his defense thereby establishing a reasonable doubt that he committed the crime. Rather than be a good Prosecutor and work on a good cross-examination for the expected evidence, Leeman is asking the court to hold his hand and stop the evidence from being presented to the jury before it even starts. It is the jury's job to find facts, and to determine which of those facts are true and which of them are not. Leeman knew that the evidence would call for a conclusion on part of the jury that there is a reasonable doubt that Miller committed the crimes, rather, the Hatchers.

"State of Indiana vs. John Miller, comes now the State and files a motion in limine seeking to prevent the defense from presenting evidence to the jury. Show the State present by Henry Leeman, the defendant present and by counsel, Gavin Palmer. Mr. Leeman, your motion is based on?" Judge Thomas said as he looked over the file.

" Huh, 31-3-54-2 your Honor, specifically that the defense intends to offer evidence regarding other crimes committed by Marvin and Alvin Hatcher, said crimes are in no way related to this crime, however, in an attempt to confuse the jury, the defense will offer into evidence a set of facts that seem similar to the facts in this case giving the impression that the Hatchers had an opportunity to commit this crime, but, the defense has no real physical evidence to establish such a claim. The State therefore prays that this court grant the States motion and for any other relief deemed necessary," Leeman said to the Judge standing behind his table.

"Mr. Palmer, your take on this?" asked the Judge.

"Well, we believe that the evidence will establish that the Hatchers did commit this crime, we further believe that the evidence will establish more than just an opportunity!"

"Do you have any physical evidence that you could offer this court that would establish support for such a theory?" Judge Thomas asked.

"Yes, there are bite marks from many cases involving the Hatchers that exactly match...."

"Again your honor, that's not real evidence, it just gives the impression that because there are bite marks in both cases, it must have been committed by the Hatchers," Leeman interrupted.

"We are checking now for matching blood samples," Palmer instructed.

"Do you have any evidence that you can offer this court now, I don't care what you're checking on, what do you have now?" Judge Thomas asked.

"I am not required to prove my case to you before it is presented to the jury; the jury is the finder of fact, not you, that's why we have a jury system, to find, and, to determine the truth of those facts presented. I would also remind you that Stevens vs. State of Indiana in the Appeals Court, and later the State Supreme Court, held that to disallow the defense from using circumstantial evidence to establish a reasonable doubt would be the same as disallowing the State to present circumstantial evidence in any given case, and, as such, the high court stated that, to do so, would violate a defendants Sixth Amendment right to a fair trial and his Fourteenth Amendment right to due process. It is simply reversible error." Palmer fired back.

"Show the motion in limine is GRANTED! Mr. Palmer, should you find further evidence that supports your theory; we will revisit this motion and reconsider the order at that time. As it stands now, the States motion in limine is hereby granted. You will not refer to any evidence regarding the testimony of a Detective Taylor, the Hatchers, or, their cases, further, you will not refer to any physical evidence in those cases whatsoever. Now, to be fair to the defense, I will continue the trial until Monday. That gives you the weekend to adjust to this court's ruling today. As I said Mr. Palmer, should your tests come back by Monday, we will revisit these issues. Judge

Thomas instructed.

Palmer got up and walked out of the court room. He went over to his office to call Detective Taylor.

"Detective Taylor, I was wondering if you could meet me at Tilly's for a drink tonight?

"Sure, be glad to Gavin."

"Say, about sevenish?"

"Great, see you there counselor."

Palmer hung up the phone and looked down to the papers on his desk. He was so pissed that he couldn't even read the print. He knew that Leeman would pull some shit, but, it was just unbelievable to think that he would do that just to win a case. This was a murder case that no doubt had death penalty possibilities. Leeman has reduced this case to underhanded backdoor deals with this ignorant Judge. Why not just enter a verdict for the jury of guilty and send him on to prison. Better yet, they could just execute him in the center of the courtroom.

Palmer wasn't going to go out like that. He reached up to a shelf and pulled down *Criminal Law and Procedure, 5th Addition.* He looked up the law regarding the filing of an appeal before the

Appeals Court in cases where a trial was still at hand in the Trial Court. Normally, you can only appeal a case that has been fully adjudicated. That is, a criminal case that has not only reached a verdict, but, a sentence has been handed down by the trial court, thereby giving the Appeals Court jurisdiction to hear the matter on appeal. The law stated;

Except as otherwise provided by the Constitution of the United States, no person shall take appeal from a case of the trial court without having satisfied the requirements of full adjudication by a verdict entered from either a judge of the lower court, or, the jury should one exist in the case. Further, it is premature to file an appeal without having been sentenced in the lower court. The exception to this rule exists only upon grounds that a ruling in the lower court before or during the trial of a defendant will substantially deny the accused a constitutional right that will affect the outcome of the verdict disfavored to the accused. The constitutional right denied should relate only to the defendants right to a fair trial. Upon receiving the notice of appeal, the lower court will stop all proceedings and turn the case over to the appeals court for review and ruling on the matter in question. Any other constitutional issues can be reviewed by the appeals court after full adjudication.

Palmer told his secretary to go get some dinner and return to the office. "It's going to be a long night," Palmer said as he started opening books and stacking them neatly on his desk. As always, he pulled out his long yellow legal pad and his fine ballpoint pen and placed them in front of him. First, he would draw up a motion known as a *Notice and request to certify the case.* This motion let the court and the Prosecutor know that the defense was going to appeal the court's decision to exclude the evidence of the Hatchers and the testimony of Detective Taylor as well as requesting the clerk to prepare a portion of the record to be forwarded with the brief of the defendant to the appeals court. Palmer started working on his brief and lost track of time. He had forgotten all about meeting Detective Taylor at Tilly's.

Detective Taylor came walking into Palmers office. "Where the hell was you, I must have got about half drunk waiting on you?"

"I'm sorry Detective; I got caught up in this case and forgot!"

"Are you working on the Star case?" Taylor said looking down at the desk.

"Yeah, I'm preparing a brief for the appeals court. Leeman filed a motion to stop me from presenting any evidence of the Hatchers or you."

"Your bullshit'n, what a coward. Well, I brought us a case of the best beer money can buy. Let me take my jacket off and help you get this done."

The two worked all night on the brief. Palmer joined Taylor in drinking a few of the beers. By five am, they were drunk.

"If I don't connect the Hatcher boys to this crime, I could be looking at the conviction of an innocent man," Palmer said leaning back on his chair.

"That's not going to happen Gavin, your too damn good for that!" Taylor said lying on the couch across from Palmers desk.

Chapter 17

The Defense of John Miller;

"ALL RISE, the Clark Superior Court in and for the 29th Judicial Circuit is now in session, the Honorable Judge Thomas presiding," said the Court Bailiff.

"Please be seated, we are on today.........the State rested their case, and we will start the defense, Mr. Palmer, is the defense prepared to move forward at this time?" the Judge asked.

"Judge the Defense moves for a directed verdict at this time and request oral argument outside the presence of the jury."

"Very well, Mr. Prosecutor?"

"We believe that we have put forth enough evidence in this case to sustain our burden of proof. We further believe that the case should be decided by the jury as the facts presented by the State are not in dispute and lead, while circumstantial, to a finding of guilty."

"The facts presented by the State do not lead to a finding of guilty by no stretch of the imagination, the State failed to prove anything other than my client had an opportunity to commit the crime, thus, the State failed to establish that the defendant committed any crime beyond a reasonable doubt," Palmer countered.

"I'm going to overrule your motion for a directed verdict and deny the motion at this time Mr. Palmer. I believe without addressing the merits of the case that the charges here are substantial and should be decided by the jury. Should you disagree with the decision handed down by the jury, you will be given an opportunity to address the court in a motion to correct errors."

"Fine Judge," Palmer answered.

"You may call your first witness Mr. Palmer," the Judge instructed.

"Defense calls Kimberly Miller to the stand."

Kim Miller got up from her seat and walked to the witness stand. Palmer grabbed a file and approached her.

"Mrs. Miller, you are the wife of the defendant is that correct?" Palmer questioned.

"Yes"

"Ok, now....on the night of January 25th of this year, can you tell the jury how it happened that your husband, the defendant, went to the Fox Club without you?"

"Yes, I sent him down there to pick up some chips for me......huh"

"Some potato chips," Palmer interrupted.

"Yes, potato chips."

"Ok and how long was he gone?"

"About 30 minutes or so."

"And was there anybody with him...., did anyone go to the bar with him that night?"

"No, he was by himself."

"Before going to the bar, how long was John at home?"

"All day."

"Now, did you ever see Abby Star the night of the 25th?"

"I've never seen Abby Star in my life."

"She was never at your house, for any reason?"

"Never!"

"Can you tell us what time he left and then returned please?"

"He left about 9:30 and returned shortly after 10:00."

"Thank you, I have nothing further of this witness," Palmer instructed.

"Mr. Prosecutor?" the judge asked.

"Yes, you're Honor." Leeman said as he approached Kim Miller.

"Mrs. Miller, would it be fair to say that you love your husband?"

"Yes, I love him very much!"

"Would it also be fair to say you would do anything to defend him?"

"Anything but lie."

"I see yes, well, is it true that you and your husband like having sex parties?"

"No, it's not true."

"So, Mrs. Miller, an officer has testified that he seen you, along with the defendant, having sex with a 19 year old girl, is it your testimony here today that that never happened?"

"No, it happened, but............."

"And so then to do so must mean that you enjoy doing it, people don't do things they don't like for fun, am I correct?"

"John didn't like it; I had to talk him into it."

"Yes, I'm sure you did!"

"OBJECTION," Palmer shouted.

"Sustained Mr. Leeman, please allow the witness to answer only questions you present," agreed the judge.

"I have nothing further for Mrs. Miller Judge," Leeman said as he took his seat.

"Mr. Palmer?"asked the Judge.

"I will redirect your Honor," Palmer said as he walked over to the jury box.

"How many times have you and the defendant had sex with a third person Mrs. Miller?

"Just that once!"

"At no other time had you had sex outside the marriage?"

"Never."

"And you were about to testify about the defendants reluctance to want to have a threesome, could you please elaborate on that?"

"John did not want to do it; we were drinking and sort of talked him in to it."

"I see, thank you. No further questions."

After questioning a few witnesses about the good character of

John Miller, the defense rested its case. The Judge then called for closing arguments. The Prosecutor walked over to the jury.

"You the jury have been called here to hear and determine the facts of this case and thereafter having decided on what is true and what is not, make a decision on the guilt or innocence of the defendant. You must find the defendant guilty beyond a reasonable doubt as to the elements of rape in count one, and murder in count two. The evidence here is undisputed. The defendant was seen at the scene of the crime, standing right where the body was found. He knew the young lady from classes he taught. He had access to the very drugs found in her system. She had the smell of beer on her, but had not been drinking. The evidence suggests that not only was the defendant drinking beer that very night, but that there was beer cans everywhere in his house. The evidence shows that the defendant has a history of enjoying sex with young girls. When I say the facts are undisputed, i mean that the defense has not put forth any excuse for any of it. Mrs. Miller testified that the defendant was home all day and was only gone 30 minutes to get her some chips. Now I ask you, should we refuse to look at the great possibility that a sex party got out of hand that night between Abby Star and the Millers thereby costing the girl her life and calling for a cover up? Do the facts not establish this? I will leave that question up to you, the jury. I ask you to return a verdict of guilty on both counts and give this family, the victim, and the town justice. Thank you."

Palmer got up and patted John Miller on the shoulder. He walked around the defense table and headed to the jury box.

"The Prosecutor was right about one thing......The victim and her family has a right to seek justice in this matter, however, justice works both ways. You see, it would not be justice to convict the wrong person for the crimes committed while the real killer remained free now would it? We are in a murder trial, one that has consequences to the defendant and his family. The evidence does not exist here. There is no physical evidence linking the defendant to this crime. There are no eye witnesses here to testify that they saw the defendant in the act. There has only been circumstantial evidence offered to suggest that the defendant had an opportunity to commit the crime, essentially, that he could have done it! That's not enough! To prove a case beyond a reasonable doubt, mere opportunity is insufficient for a conviction. If one were to look hard enough, we could find that just about everyone in that bar had the opportunity to commit this crime. A man's life now sets before you. I implore you to make the right decision in this matter. The defense asks that you set the record straight and return a verdict of not guilty in this matter. Let's send this innocent man home and look for the real killers, justice for the victim and her family.   Thank you."

"Thank you Mr. Palmer. The case is now in your hands. As the Judge I ask you to decide this case by the instruction you have been given. The jury will now be sent to deliberations. Thank you," the Judge said as pointed to the jury room.

Palmer turned to John Miller. "It's probably going to be a couple of days before they make a decision John. I will be in touch." Palmer gathered his things and met Detective Taylor at the door.

"How about a late lunch on me Detective?" Palmer asked.

"I thought you would never ask Gavin," Detective Taylor replied.

They men left for the restaurant to get a bite to eat. After their meal, they decided to have a drank to relieve the stress of the trial.

One hour turned into four. The waitress came over to Palmer.

"Mr. Palmer, there's a call for you at the register Sir."

"Ok, thank you." Palmer walked over and got on the phone. "Hello, Gavin Palmer here!"

"Gavin, there's a verdict," said Palmers secretary.

"Already, wow," Palmer said in shock. "Ok, I'm on my way now."

Palmer hung the phone up and headed back to his table. "We got a verdict Detective!"

"Well, looks like you added a win to all those others Gavin," Detective Taylor said in excitement. Detective Taylor has been around long enough to know that a quick verdict is almost always a not-guilty. The two headed out for the courthouse.

The Judge saw that all the parties had arrived and called for the jury.

"Mr. Jury foreperson, would you please stand, the Defendant will rise for the reading of the verdict," ordered the Judge.

"In the matter of the State of Indiana vs. John Miller, what say you?"

"In the matter of State vs. John Miller, as to count one, rape, we find the defendant guilty."

The courtroom erupted. Palmer put his head down.

"As to count two, murder in the first degree, guilty as charged!"

"Thank you, the jury is thanked for its service and you are now excused." The jury went out through the Jury room.

"Mr. Miller, you have been convicted by a jury of you peers. It will be the sentence of this court that you receive the penalty of death by lethal injection. You are remanded to the Sheriff of Clark County awaiting to be transported to the Indiana Department of Correction where you will serve your sentence...........God help your soul."

"Defense will appeal the case your Honor," Palmer said still stunned by the verdict.

"So noted Mr. Palmer."

A Sheriff came up and put John Miller in hand cuffs. He was escorted away and everyone left the courtroom. Palmer just set at the defense table looking blank. Detective Taylor waited outside the courtroom door for Palmer. After about ten minutes, he opened the door to the empty courtroom and seen Palmer setting at the table not moving. Detective Taylor closed the door and went on back to his hotel room.

Chapter 18

Palmer had filed an appeal before the State Appeals Court. He cited the fact that there was no evidence against John Miller and that the Appeals Court should reverse the case and vacate the judgment of the lower court. He also appealed the decision of Judge Thomas to keep the jury from hearing evidence of the Hatchers. The Court of Appeals decided the case in a three part decision. Essentially, they stated that they would not reweigh the evidence and that the State met its burden in proving its case. As to the Hatchers, the Appeals court decided that there was no prejudicial effect because the defense had an opportunity to establish that the evidence to be offered had "evidentiary value". Put plainly, the appeal was denied. Palmer appealed that decision to the Supreme Court and they refused to hear the case.

Judge Thomas was at the bench waiting on Gavin Palmer to show up for a court case. It was not like Palmer to be late for a pending case. The Judge decided to hear other cases while waiting on Palmer to show. He never did.

"Call over to Palmers office and find out what is taking him so long," Judge Thomas ordered of his Court Bailiff.

The Bailiff walked in to her office and got on the phone;

"Yes, Judge Thomas is waiting on Gavin; he has a case in court and is not here?"

"He has not been in to the office for three days," said Palmers secretary.

"Ok, I will inform the Judge, thank you."

"They have not seen Gavin in three days Judge," said the Bailiff.

"Very well, I am going to continue this case until the 10th."

"Judge Thomas got up and told the Bailiff to continue all the cases on the roster for that day."I have got to go somewhere this afternoon," he said as he reached for coat.

Judge Thomas started thinking about the last time he seen Palmer. It was at the trial of John Miller. He went down and got in his car.

He drove over to Palmers house and as he got out he noticed a lot of mail in the mail box. He knocked on the door several times but didn't get an answer.

"GAVIN, you there?"

Judge Thomas looked around back to see if he might be in the back yard or the garage. He didn't see anything there. He got into his car and drove off.

The reports were flooding the airways and papers regarding the denial of John Millers appeal. John Miller had been moved to the Maximum Security Prison in Indiana where they housed death row inmates. The people in Clark County talked about how the Baby Killer (John Miller) had leaded a double life for all those years. John's parents had moved their medical practice to another location in Indiana due to the lack of clients. Eventually, they moved out of Clark County themselves.

When word of the disappearance of Gavin Palmer had spread, most people said he was embarrassed to show his face in town. That the once great Criminal Defense Attorney would be no more. The few that believed that John Miller was innocent, and there were a few, believed that Gavin Palmer was devising a great plan to get John Miller out of jail and out of trouble. One day, the Law Offices of Gavin Palmer were being cleaned out. The building remained empty for a long time.

Chapter 19

6 Years later; June 1989

Beyond the great wall of the State Prison was a narrow hall that took the public in to an observation room. The hall had a constant cold breeze flowing even though the summer heat of Indiana was intense that evening. The feeling was uneasy as the environment had a hint of darkness and set a mood of hopelessness. The observation room had several church like wood benches that faced a large pale of glass. Inside the glass housed a hospital bed with all kinds of gadgets and tubes set to one side. The execution chamber had a phone and intense lighting so that the observer could clearly see that justice was being accomplished. In 3 hours, John Miller would meet his fate.

Outside the walls, a group of reporters were gathered to give their reports on the execution. Next to them were a large group of protesters holding signs that read, "stop the killing". The protesters were protesting against executions in general, rather than a plea for the innocence of John Miller.

John Miller has been housed on death row for nearly 7 years now. He lived in a 4x4 metal cell that housed only a metal bunk and an area to go to the bathroom. It was a blank existence with no windows to see the earth's finer pleasures. There was nothing to do but read. Many death row inmates would spend their days and years working on their legal cases in an attempt to save their lives. After being denied by every court in the nation, they would turn to a way out. They would set and think of a way to end their lives thus, to escape the hell and torcher of death row.

"Mr. Miller, you have your last visit, please stand and turn around to be cuffed!" said a guard.

John Miller was escorted to a secured visiting room with a large glass in which to see the visitors and a phone in which to communicate. As he entered, he saw that his mom could not hold back the tears. His father had a blank look about him as if he were in a severe state of shock. John knew that this visit would be the hardest thing he has ever done. He tried to comfort his parents by explaining that this was a way out, and that it was what had to happen to spare him from the hell he faced every day and the shame he felt from being cast as a baby killer. As the visit ended, John's parents slowly exited the room so that Johns wife Kim could come in. As they walked out, John held is hand to the glass. His Father stopped to look back; he then walked back to the glass and put his hand to the other side. No further words were exchanged.

John's parents waited outside the visiting room for Kim as she visited John for the last time. They could hear the screams and cries from Kim in the visiting room. It would be a moment they would never forget.

With tears flooding his face, John was escorted back to his cell where he would wait another hour for his ticket out. As he set on the edge of the bunk, he tried to think about all the good times he had. He remembered his childhood and all the fun he had with his first car. He thought about his college days and all the friends he met. He thought about Kim and how much he loved her. John made peace with himself and accepted that life was not fare. His last thought as he heard guards coming down the hall to get him were "No one will ever know I was innocent."

The guards opened the door and shackled John up. They pointed to the direction of the execution chambers and John began to walk. He entered the room and was told to lie down on the bed. He heard a scream from the observation room and looked to see Kim with her hand over her mouth running out of the room. John could not hold back the emotions. The guard went to grab Johns arm to strap it for the insertion of needles and John pulled away. The guard stopped and watched. John held two fingers expressing the piece sign. At 12:02 am, John Miller was pronounced dead.

Chapter 20

2 Years later; July 5th, 1991

Palmer got out of bed as the alarm sounded. He walked into the kitchen to start the coffee pot he pre-set the night before. As the coffee began to brew, he turned on the small TV in the kitchen and took a seat at the kitchen table. The morning news was interviewing a brilliant lawyer who was explaining the term of DNA and how it could be used in criminal trials. He went on to say that he had sought exoneration of his client and could establish proof by way of DNA.

"The samples of blood taken from the crime scene, as well as hair and other samples secured by the Police at the time of the incident point to someone other than my client. If we had a sample of the real killers DNA, we could positively identify the killer by the vary use of the DNA."

Palmers head tilted to the left as he continued to watch the story of this huge breakthrough in criminal evidence. He snatched up a cup of coffee and went to grab the phone.

"This is Gavin Palmer; I would like to speak to Detective Taylor please!"

"One moment Mr. Palmer, I will see if he's in."

Detective Taylor came on.

"Well Gavin, I'm going to take a shot in the dark here and say you are calling me about the Abby Star case?"

"Yes, I am Detective."

"And I'm willing to bet all the horses in Kentucky that you have found out about the new DNA and want me to run samples on the evidence we retained?"

Palmer was speechless; it was like Taylor had read his mind.

"Don't worry my ole friend, we sent the samples out a week ago and I got them back today. The DNA matches the Hatcher Brothers. I was going to call, but I wanted to get the results back first, I am overnighting the results to you as we speak," Taylor said with excitement.

"You have truly been a good friend Detective, truly.........," Palmer said with increasing emotions.

"No problem Gavin, it's what we do. I just wish that we could have done this before the execution. I was sorry to hear that it went through."

"Well, it looks like I have a motion to file Detective!"

"Duty calls Gavin, duty calls......"

Palmer got another cup of coffee and walked down the hall to his study. He took a seat at the desk and with all the air he could muster, blew the dust back from his typewriter. He began typing.

The next day, Court Bailiff Carroll Deeds was opening the door to her office at the Clark Superior Court. All of a sudden she felt the presence of someone standing behind her.

"Gavin, is that you? She asked.

"I have a motion to file," Palmer replied.

"Yes of course, please come in, I will get the file stamper ready for you."

Palmer stamped the motion and handed to the Bailiff. She took the motion and headed for the Judge's chambers.

"You're never going to guess who just came in and filed a motion Judge?"

"F. Lee Baily?" Judge Thomas said as he laughed aloud.

"No, Gavin Palmer!"

"Really, let's take a look at it." Judge Thomas looked over the paperwork and the evidence of the DNA. The more he read, the worse he began to feel.

"Oh my god, ohhhh my god," the Judge said.

The Judge entered an order for the Prosecutor to respond to the motion calling for the exoneration of John Miller within 10 days. The State filed no response.

Palmer heard a knock at the door. As he opened the door, he noticed Judge Thomas's car parked in the driveway.

"I wanted to bring this order to you personally Gavin, and I want you to know how truly bad I feel, that poor boy lost his life because of my foolish rulings, I have not been able to sleep for days," said the Judge as he handed the white piece of paper over to Palmer. Palmer took the order and nodded. He shut the door without saying a word. Once back inside, he looked at the order, it read;

ORDER OF THE COURT

Counsel having filed herein a motion for an order seeking to exonerate John Miller, and the State having been given a chance to respond, court now finds sufficient evidence exists that John Miller did not commit the crimes of rape and murder, the convictions entered by judgment shall be forever lifted, and the Clerk of this Court is hereby ordered to enter a not-guilty finding by this court as to all charges. Be it so ordered. S/ Judge Thomas.

Palmer rolled the order up and got his keys off the coffee table. He drove to the cemetery and got out of his car. He started walking through the tombstones and noticed to his right a big brown headstone. He walked up to it and nodded his head. It read;

Jonathan C. Matts 1942-1983

He walked around to an open area and began to walk up to a white headstone, it read;

John D. Miller 1968-1991

Palmer reached into his coat pocket and pulled out the order given to him by Judge Thomas. He pulled a few weeds from around the stone and placed it in the center of the tombstone and walked away.

Clark Superior Court is now in session, Judge Thomas presiding;

"Son, do you have an Attorney to represent you today?" Judge Thomas asked.

The big doors opened;

"Gavin Palmer for the defense your Honor!"

Look for my next novel; Next of Kin coming in the winter of 2011.

David Alex Fleming

Dying Innocence

Author Note's

It is both my honor and pleasure to write *Dying Innocence*. I write my first novel in tribute to the people who lost their lives having been falsely accused of such horrific unspeakable acts. It is true that the story of John Miller is fictional, that is, the persons, characters, places, and incidents recorded herein are all the product of my imagination, it is also true that the story was written based on the existence of non-fictional facts, thus, it is based on true actual events that are now apparent of our past. It was necessary, given the circumstances here, to use fiction as a way to demonstrate what has happened in the past to others whose names we may never know.

I am reminded of the writings of Rachel Carson when she stated," The subject chooses the writer rather than the writer choosing the subject." I cannot tell you how true that is for me as it relates to this book. When I think of the plight of these people, I can think of no other story that needs to be told. I intended to write this novel as a non-fictional work. I wanted to go back in history, discover cases where people have been executed based on eye-witness testimony, examine the same evidence using the DNA technologies of today, find those who were indeed innocent, and clear their names while at the same time writing my findings for the world to see. It was never enough to just write their stories, I wanted to see that history was changed and justice was accomplished. In a perfect world, this may have been possible. After a time consuming research project that reviewed five cases from the past, I was faced with the reality that once the defendants were executed, the DNA evidence necessary to complete our task was destroyed along with all the other physical evidence in the case.

As I said before, the subject of this book had already been chosen, it was merely the question of which way it was to be written. I chose to write it as a fictional novel but I am in hopes that when you read it, you will in vision the fact that somewhere in our pasts, there were many John Miller's that didn't get to tell their story. I would have loved to be able to do that for them.

If you are wondering why I seem to take it personally, I would say this; can you imagine being accused of a rape and murder, persecuted in the public and prosecuted in the courts. Having to set there and watch an eye witness point the finger at you, be shamed by your own family, set on death row for ten years, and then walked to your death as you swore to the end you didn't do it. It bothers me much I do admit. I wonder at times if I am the only one who thinks of these people. I must assume that the last thing they thought to themselves before being executed was, "No one will ever know I was innocent." If this novel brings these events to your attention, then at least in a general way, we will have known that some of them were innocent, even if we never know their names.

I am also mindful of the fact that there are people serving life in prison or who are on death row having been convicted upon eye witness testimony that could not benefit from the science of DNA for reasons that DNA was not a factor in their case. Either none was left or found at the crime scene, or, it simply did not apply to their case due to the type of crime being charged. They may very well be reading this book. To them I say, NEVER GIVE UP!!!

I could not write a book of this nature without honoring Attorney Barry Scheck and members of the Innocence Project. If it were not for these talented people, hundreds if not thousands of people would have lost their lives to the same fate as all the John Millers. I can't respect Barry and his team enough. What a great legal mind of our time. Truly God Sent.

I hope you have enjoyed reading my first novel. I hope you have had as much excitement reading it as I had writing it. While it should be noted that some parts of the book were bothersome to research and write, it was exciting to be able to tell the stories of these people, even if it had to be done in fiction. Please visit me at; www.davidalexfleming.webs.com and let me know what you thought of the book. There is a link provided to my e-mail. I respond to everyone, however, I do not open attachments. You will also find a link to the Innocence Project should you wish to donate your time or money. It is a great cause.

About the Author

David Alex Fleming is the penname for David W. Nethercutt. Mr. Nethercutt lives in Indiana. He has four children, Amanda, Emma, Ashton and Skyler of whom this book would not been possible. My children are the reflection in my eye and the air that I breath.

Made in the USA
Charleston, SC
01 April 2011